Inverness Square

Inverness Square

Rose Boucheron

PIATKUS

For more information on other books
published by Piatkus, visit our website at
www.piatkus.co.uk

Copyright © 2001 by Rose Boucheron

First published in Great Britain in 2001 by
Judy Piatkus (Publishers) Ltd of
5 Windmill Street, London W1T 2JA
email:info@piatkus.co.uk

The moral right of the author has been asserted

A catalogue record for this book is available from the British Library

ISBN 0 7499 0568 9

Set in Times by
Action Publishing Technology Ltd, Gloucester

Printed and bound in Great Britain by
Butler & Tanner Ltd, Frome, Somerset

For my children

Chapter One

1939

When the last sonorous peal of Big Ben rang out at the end of 1938, a huge sigh of relief could almost be heard.

What a year it had been with the threat of war uppermost in everyone's mind, to be finally relieved in September with Neville Chamberlain waving his little bit of paper – 'it is to be peace in our time . . .' Well, that had been history-making and now with the excitement and euphoria of a New Year, everything was going to be great, a bright new year to look forward to.

Nineteen thirty-nine was enjoying a wonderful spring, coming in so quickly after a long winter; it was March and a host of daffodils had unfurled their buds and the plane trees had erupted with the sudden onslaught of warm breezes and sunshine; every growing thing was taken by surprise.

In Balmoral Street all the back gardens held lines of washing billowing in the breeze. The chimneys had ceased to belch coal smoke; housewives polished their brass door knockers and blackleaded the coal-hole cover until it looked like silver.

Julie (christened Juliet Rose) Halliwell, in her last term at school, positively danced along, arm in arm with

1

Gwen, her best friend, leaving her at the corner of Sundawn Road with Gwen promising to call for her to go to the library early that evening.

Through the brass letter box, she pulled the string which connected it to the latch, and the door sprang open.

'Mum – it's me!' Hanging her school satchel on the row of hooks she went into the kitchen to see her mother collecting a pile of ironed washing from the clothes airer she had stood out to air in the sun.

'Mum, can I go to the library with Gwen after tea?'

'Yes, all right, I thought they closed Wednesday.'

'They used to, but it's changed now.'

Not that her mother would know, she never went to the library, that beautiful and elegant old house which had been taken over by the council, an eighteenth-century house with magnificent ceilings and woodwork. The people of the area were extremely fortunate to have such a library, left to them by a beneficent old man who had lived in the area since Victorian times. Julie thought she would like to live in a house like that when she got married. If she got married. She wasn't sure yet. She had a whole lot of living to do before that. Besides, it wasn't a good idea for an actress to marry – she would meet so many boys . . .

'Get on with your tea then,' Mrs Halliwell said. 'I made a fruit cake yesterday. It's always better the day after.'

'Mmm, lovely.' Julie put the kettle back on the range where it began to sing loudly at once.

She grabbed a magazine from the rack, *Picture Play* – an American magazine her mother sometimes allowed her to buy from the second-hand bookstall in the market. In the motion picture mags, as they were called in

America, Julie got all her information about what was going on in Hollywood: who was who in the film world. It was her favourite subject, much to Mrs Halliwell's regret.

Julie spread jam on the newly baked bread and, licking her sticky fingers, flicked through the pages avidly. She had decided that when she left school she was going to be an actress. (She would change her name to Lucille, for apparently that was Joan Crawford's real name.) Lucille la Soeur she had been christened. Her mother wouldn't be best pleased, but she needn't know – anybody could change their name if they wanted to and Lucille Halliwell sounded quite good. Or something royal perhaps – Lucille Marlborough, or Buckingham, or Windsor . . .

And here was a full-page picture of Greta Garbo! Oh, to look like her! She surely must be the most beautiful girl in the world. That long narrow mouth; Julie unconsciously twisted hers and stretched it – that fall of sleek shining hair, that beautiful straight nose and those eyes! Oh, so deep-set with the longest eyelashes you've ever seen. Surely they couldn't be false as Gwen suspected. Gwen was unromantic – you could just tell they were real.

Julie hurried over to the dresser and stared into the tiny mirror. She couldn't have looked more different. Thick fair hair, inclined to curl, strong and wayward, while you could see Garbo's was fine, like silk . . . Then her nose was, well, anyhow, and her eyes, a funny colour, a sort of washed-out blue, not deep set, just plonked on to her face. One day she would buy some eyeblack and when her mother was out paint her lashes, and she would put it on so thick . . . Her heart began to beat faster at the very thought of it.

In this American magazine, it said Maybelline was the

3

best and there was a picture of a girl in the advert. She would bet that was Ann Southern with the longest lashes; still, she couldn't afford that. But when she began earning, that was another thing.

She would not go to work in Randall and Philipps, she was adamant about that. Even if it was in the office. Imagine, just walking down to the main road, and along a bit and then turning into the factory entrance! And someone had told her you had to clock on! She clutched her heart theatrically. Never; she would rather die!

She sighed deeply and cut herself a slice of rich fruit cake. One thing about her mum, she was a good cook – not like Gwen's mum who couldn't even cook a potato.

Finishing off another slice, she sat back, feeling full. She shouldn't have had that second piece. Still . . . Here on the next page was Marlene. She quickly turned it over; she couldn't bear Marlene Dietrich – who did she think she was? Just a poor copy of Garbo, that's what . . . but oh, look at Clark Gable! He did look a bit old, but that smile . . . And Robert Taylor now, with that wicked look in his eyes . . . It was just as if he was looking straight at her, cigarette dangling from that beautiful mouth – 'chiselled' they called it – looking just as if it was carved out of marble. She sighed and was about to press the picture to her lips when her mother walked in.

'Well, that's that, then,' she said, taking the folded clothes upstairs. 'When are you going—'

'Gwen's calling for me.' She took out her plate and cup, rinsed them under the tap; and put the tea things away. Her father would be home at five thirty, having walked the mile from the factory as he did every day.

All the streets in that part of South London looked pretty much the same. Most of them were lined with plane trees, and on either side were rows of terraced

Victorian or Edwardian houses all built to see better days. Sometimes intersected by a small street which had no trees, the houses were solidly built with impressive marble fireplaces in the two main rooms downstairs, and a kitchen and scullery. Upstairs three bedrooms and no bathroom. Bathing was done in the large bath which hung outside on the wall, to be brought in on Friday evenings, and the lavatory was outside. The Halliwells were lucky enough to have a large flat round bath, from when Julie's father had decided to keep ducks for the eggs, until her mother said she heard they were dangerous; but they did keep the bath – which was better, Julie thought, than the old deep oval galvanised ones that hung outside next door on the Taylors' wall. The small garden, Bob Halliwell's pride and joy, held a small lilac and laburnum tree and in the autumn, asters and dahlias. A few chickens scrabbled about in the small chicken run beneath the laburnum tree, scratching in the black London soil which still held some nourishment.

The mangle stood outside too, and some men had put up a small shed, but because they kept chickens, Julie's father had a hen-house. Most of the houses had been made into flats, the third bedroom being turned into a kitchen, but the Halliwells were fortunate to have it all to themselves. Old Mrs Halliwell, Bob's mother, had rented the house to bring up her brood, and when her son married had passed on the tenancy to her eldest son, the landlord being agreeable, she having been such a good tenant. Twenty years, and never a penny owing. A record, he told himself, more than he could say for some. But then, poor devils, the Depression had made more than a difference in their lives. Even Bob Halliwell, as honest a workman as you would find, had gone through two years of being out of work and on the dole. Not much anyone could do about it.

They were much worse off up north, they said, and in desperate cases they had relief, but no one wanted to accept that. It was like taking charity. Now, thank God, things had been on the mend for some years, although, the landlord told himself, he would be glad when they stopped talking about another war. No one needed that, especially those who had been through the last one . . .

'Eileen's coming home at the weekend,' Mrs Halliwell said. Eileen was her elder daughter, who worked in London. 'In an office,' she was often heard saying proudly, 'Shell Mex on the Embankment – but she's a clever girl, got a scholarship and everything.' She lived in a YWCA hostel, much to Julie's shame, who couldn't think of anything worse. But she did come home some weekends – more's the pity, Julie thought. She didn't much like her sister. Eileen was old-fashioned, no style about her; she read clever books and studied, and had a very good job. They thought the world of her, the management, Mrs Halliwell said. Her mother did too, and wished Julie was more like her.

Julie's lip curled, thinking of her with her old-fashioned clothes, her hat pulled straight, and not a scrap of make-up on – even when she could. At twenty-one she could do what she liked, but there'd never been sight of any boyfriend. But Eileen never occupied much of Julie's thoughts; she had much more important things to think about.

The knocker went and she took down her books from the dresser and ran to the door. 'Coming!'

'Now, don't be late!' Mrs Halliwell called. 'Back here by half-past six.'

'I know!' Julie cried and, bright-eyed, joined her friend Gwen.

*

6

All the workers were coming home about now. Mr Forsdyke from up the road passed Julie and touched his cap politely. Mr Forsdyke was a foreman, and was ever such a gentleman, while Mrs Forsdyke, who came, they said, from somewhere in South-west London, Wimbledon, you might know, was quite someone. South London was different, although Julie firmly believed that Balmoral Street was the best of the lot. After all, it was a royal name, everyone knew that.

Billy Webb was leaning over the iron gate, smoking and grinning at them. Gwen blushed.

'Come on, don't take any notice of him, they're a rum crowd, those Webbs, my mother says. Doris, his sister, is getting married at Easter – and not before time, my mother said. I heard her say so to Mrs Gathergood.'

'Oh, Julie you are awful. You shouldn't say things like that. After all—'

'Oh, come on, let's cross over. I can't stand that silly Ivy Woods. She always wants to stop and talk – honestly . . .'

But half-way up the road, she began to dawdle, and Gwen knew why. On the corner where a small side street bisected Balmoral Street stood quite an impressive shop – an off licence, much patronized by the locals of the area. In that shop lived Lesley Daly, the son of the widowed Irish proprietress, Ada Beatrice Daly; her name was painted over the door for all the world to see.

Her step consciously slower, Gwen could feel Julie's arm grabbing hers, as, head held high, she went out of her way not to look across at the shop.

'He's there,' whispered Gwen. 'In the shop . . .'

It was as much as Julie could do not to look across the road.

'He's looking over this way,' Gwen said, her dimple showing.

7

'As if I care,' Julie said, but her heart was thumping wildly. For she was in love with Les Daly – had been ever since she could remember. Now, her pretty face was flushed as she slowed down her speed, and tried her hardest not to turn around.

'Did he see us?' she whispered.

''Course he did! Could hardly miss us!' and they giggled and hurried on until they came to the corner of the road and turned into the library.

Cooking her husband's tea, Nancy Halliwell's thoughts were all on Julie and what would happen to her when she left school. She seemed to want to do all sorts of silly things, instead of trying to better herself and work in an office – acting, hairdressing, floristry, if you please! To work in a shop? Where, might one ask, would that lead?

Of course, you could bet that Gwen Edwards would find herself a good job, her dad would see to that. Nancy quite liked Gwen, she was a nice little thing, quiet and unassuming, a really good friend to Julie. But her family. Ugh. Her father, Vic Edwards, was a good-looking man, handsome in fact, and had reached a somewhat superior position on the council because of his socialist activities.

'Don't you like Mr Edwards?' she recalled Julie asking one day.

'Why do you ask that? He's all right.'

'You always have a funny look on your face when I mention Gwen's dad.'

Not without good reason, Nancy thought. Pulling strings, a lively member of the socialist party – Nancy had no time for that. True blue conservative, she had been brought up on the other side of the water and they were a conservative stronghold there. Bob now, her husband, was easygoing, too easygoing sometimes;

he wasn't much bothered about anything to do with politics; such a good-natured man.

She slipped the cooked vegetables and meat into a large dish and put it in the oven to keep warm.

No, she had reason to 'pull a face', as Julie called it. When Bob had been on relief, it had been Vic Edwards who came round to enquire into their financial position – if you could call it that. Out of work two years, on the dole – and everyone round here knew what that meant. In desperation they had had to go on relief for six months; even now it could bring a flush to her face. And of course it had to be Vic Edwards enquiring into their position.

'Course, he'd got a better job now. And that wife of his – so stuck up, and for no reason.

Still she must be fair. It had nothing to do with Gwen. In any case, Gwen would be leaving school at Easter when Julie did.

She glanced up at the clock. They should be back presently. Bob had stopped off to collect his boots from the repairers, otherwise he was always in by this time.

She heard the letter box go. Then the door opened and Bob came in.

'Ah, there you are, tea's all ready.'

Having washed himself at the kitchen sink Bob sat down to his tea. 'Where's Julie?'

'She's due back any minute, gone to the library with Gwen.'

She frowned. 'You know, Bob, we shall have to think seriously about what she'll do when she leaves school at Easter . . .'

'Oh, she'll be all right.'

'You keep saying that, but it's her future we've got to think of.'

He turned a puzzled face to hers. 'I don't know what you mean, Nan – don't the school help out there?'

'Not so as you'd notice,' she said. 'You see, Bob, although she's done a bit of shorthand and typing like Gwen at that Central school, she doesn't really know how to do it. I mean, she hated shorthand, and as for typing – swears she's not going to do it.'

'Well, then, she won't,' he said, laying down his knife and fork. 'Does she have to go into an office?'

'No, but it would be nice, Bob. I've always wanted her to have a real job like Eileen – if only ...'

'But she's not like Eileen, she's clever in other directions.'

'Like what?'

'Well, she's sort of artistic – she can act, she loves books, she's clever with her hands ...'

'You'll be saying next she ought to be a dressmaker.'

'No, I'm not—'

'What I am saying is,' she continued reasonably, 'she won't qualify for a job at Randalls, for a secretarial job, I mean; she'd have to be some filing clerk or something. I know because I spoke to one of the mothers—'

The door latch pulled, and it was Julie. 'I'm back, Mum!' and they heard her putting her hat and coat on the hatstand.

'Hello, Dad!' she said as she came in. Julie loved her father; he never bossed her around or told her what to do, and she knew she was his favourite.

'Got your books?'

'Yes, three; that should keep me going for a bit.' She sat down and poured herself a cup of tea.

'What's Gwen going to do when she leaves school, does she say?'

'Oh, I don't know – her father will find her something.

She's quite keen to go into an office – ugh.' She shuddered.

Nancy threw a knowing glance at Bob, but he lowered his eyes.

'Something will turn up,' he said.

Typical, Nancy thought.

When Julie had gone to bed, Bob turned to Nancy. 'You know what the talk is in the shop?' The factory was always referred to as the shop.

'No, what?' she asked turning her knitting round.

'War,' he said briefly. 'Everyone's on about it. Talk about us going to be evacuated up north.'

'Bob! Whatever next! We've only just got over the last one!'

'Be that as it may,' Bob said. 'But I've got a funny idea that it might come about.'

'But Chamberlain said—'

'Oh, you can't trust politicians. They say what they want to say one minute and something else the next.'

'Oh my goodness, whatever would happen if there was another war!' Nancy cried, putting down her knitting.

'Well, you can lay odds that if there are enough rumours there's something behind it. Young Eileen mentioned as much when she came on Sunday.'

'But she wouldn't know, would she?'

'She hears things in that job, you know.'

Nancy sighed. 'Well, I'm not going to worry about it. The main thing on my mind just now is Julie and you know how pig-headed she can be. I just wish she would be sensible like Gwen.'

'But Gwen has a father who can help her get a good job, I expect. Nothing I can do for Julie except at the shop.'

'She's not going there, Bob, and that's that.'

So saying, the subject was closed.

On a rare warm and sunny day in March, Nancy stood outside the newsagent's reading the advertisement cards and was struck by one which caught her eye.

WANTED: YOUNG SCHOOL LEAVER TO ASSIST IN SHOP IN EXCHANGE FOR FULL TRAINING IN ALL ASPECTS OF OFFICE WORK. TYPING, SHORTHAND, DUPLICATING. EXCELLENT OPPORTUNITY. FOR FURTHER PARTICULARS APPLY:

MR J. LEEDS
332 OLD DOVER ROAD
S.E.

Nancy read it over and over again, knowing full well that Julie would not be in the slightest bit interested. But it did sound like an opportunity. Of course, it didn't say anything about wages or what kind of shop it was, but something told her it was worth following up – that is, if she could get Julie to listen to her.

She hurried home as fast as her legs would carry her knowing exactly what Julie's reply would be. Still, it was worth a try; who knew what might come out of it?

Chapter Two

Today being Friday Nancy had it all worked out. Of course, she couldn't drag the girl there, and she fully realised what Julie's reaction would be. Still, she felt that even if Julie refused she would go herself and enquire what it was all about. It wasn't far, after all – a walk up to the top road until she got to the Angle and left into the Old Dover Road.

But her pace slowed as on reflection she wondered just exactly what it entailed? Shop? What sort of shop? A baker's shop? A toy shop? It couldn't be a grocer's. She couldn't rightly remember what the row of shops were. Bob would be dead against it – 'sounds suspicious to me,' he'd say and yet anyone who ran an office must be reliable.

She pushed open the iron gate and let herself in the front door.

Julie came home to lunch and so did Bob as a rule, but he wasn't coming home today, there was a meeting at the factory and she had cut him sandwiches. She found her heart beating quite fast with trepidation and excitement when she heard Julie come in, her light bright eyes dancing as they tended to do nowadays with the school term drawing to its close.

Julie flung down her school satchel and flopped into a chair. 'It was so hot in the playground today. We had to find a shady corner.'

'Yes, beautiful weather,' Nancy agreed. It was so nice to have Julie in a good mood and she dreaded spoiling it, but knew she would.

She began to lay the table. 'I was down at the shops today looking at Lytton's notice board—' but Julie had opened a magazine. Nancy carried on getting out plates and knives and forks and a loaf of bread.

'Anyway there was this advertisement – very interesting . . .' She waited.

Julie looked up. 'What did it say?'

'Someone advertising for a school leaver.' Now she knew she had Julie's interest. 'It said school leaver wanted to help in shop, in exchange for complete training in office work.'

Julie's face was a study. 'What?'

'I know, I know, Julie, it's not what you wanted, but it seemed a good idea. I don't know what sort of a shop it is—'

'A shop selling office equipment,' Julie said flatly and returned to her magazine.

'Put that down for a minute and listen to me,' Nancy said firmly and Julie knew by her voice that she was serious.

Wearing an uninterested look of boredom, eyes half closed, she folded her arms.

'I don't think it was selling office equipment, it didn't read like that. I just thought – well, what an opportunity—'

'For someone, I daresay,' Julie said.

'Please don't be rude. It's in the Old Dover Road. Wouldn't be far to go every day, and I thought if we

14

went along there tomorrow—'

'What? *Go* there? *Mum*! That's the *last* thing I want to do.'

'Look, you've got to do something, and you don't want this and you don't want that. Well, I can tell you, there is no way you are going into hairdressing or acting or anything else so ridiculous, so tomorrow I shall go and you will come with me.'

'I won't!' Julie went out of the door and swiftly closed it behind her.

Nancy dished up the vegetables and meat and put a cover over them to keep warm. Then, going to the door, she called out, 'Julie, your dinner's on the table,' and waited.

Presently Julie came back in. She looked pale, and Nancy felt a momentary pang of pity for her. It was so wonderful to be young and on the threshold of life, and yet there were so many difficulties to overcome. A mistake made now could follow you all your life.

They ate in silence, then Julie pushed her meal away half eaten. Nancy took no notice.

'There's apple tart, but I thought we'd save it for tonight when Dad comes home.' She knew Julie wouldn't want it.

'No, thanks.' Julie got up and washed her hands at the kitchen sink then went into the hall, where Nancy saw her combing her hair by the mirror.

'I'm off now,' she said. 'See you later.' And that was that.

Nancy gave a great sigh. What were they going to do with her?

When Bob came in that evening, she told him, but he brushed the whole idea to one side.

'If she doesn't want office work, Nan, what's the point?'

'Because she needs to get a job, and this thing is quite different.'

'But you don't know what the shop is. It could be anything. I don't like the sound of it, Nan.'

But for once Nancy dug her heels in. 'Well, I shall go over tomorrow and take Julie with me. Make an outing of it, go to that little parade of shops – she'll like that.'

Bob would never understand the ways of women. It all sounded very mysterious to him, and given his choice there was no way he would have followed it through.

Come the morning, Nancy was dressed ready to go out. She noticed that Julie had brushed her hair carefully and put her best coat on. Relieved, she thought, 'So she's thought better of it.'

'You look nice,' she said. 'I thought we'd look at the shops, go into that little café on the corner of Delacourt Road.'

But there was mutiny in the blue eyes and a set to Julie's chin that Nancy recognized. She sighed inwardly. She supposed she was being ridiculous, but there was something about the notice that drew her. After all, they did not have to go in if they didn't like the look of it.

Bob was in the garden feeding the chickens. 'We're off now, love, we won't be long.'

'You be careful,' he said. He didn't go along with the idea at all.

They walked up to the main Charlton Road, past the Victorian houses and the entrance to the Blackheath Golf Club. Julie was taller now than Nancy herself. She was so proud of her. She was pretty too, prettier than Eileen, she had to admit. But she was a worry, a worry as Eileen had never been.

When they reached the Angle Green they turned left and began to walk up the Old Dover Road. Nancy was enjoying herself; she so seldom went out of her area. Often when the girls were small she would wheel the pram to Greenwich Park or across the Heath, but she had not been this way for a long time.

'I can't get used to that new Roxy being there,' she said. 'Perhaps we should go some time, it's better than that awful fleapit on the lower road.'

They came to an expensive-looking florist's shop and a rather nice milliner's, and Julie perked up, unable to hide her interest in the lovely hats in the window and the silk stockings, finer than cobwebs, and then the chemist with its make-up and coloured bottles. It made a change from their own shops, being in a much more classy area. There were quite a few shops on the parade and further along they came to one divided in two and double fronted. It was called J. LEEDS AND SONS and a flush came to Nancy's face.

'There it is,' she whispered, feeling more than embarrassed, almost as if she were trespassing. 'Look, Julie.' As they got closer they saw that one window held everything to do with office supplies while the other was full of bits and pieces of antique furniture. Julie stifled a giggle, and Nancy was mortified. What had she expected?

'That's not it, surely,' she said reading the name above the door. 'It's not at all what I imagined.' Julie was absorbed in the window with its crimson velvet chair, the paintings on the wall, a basket of odds and ends, plates hanging on the rail, a table laid with china, while Nancy stared at the other window. It was full of office stationery, and through the open door you could see an office at the back with what she supposed was a duplicating machine. All very efficient: LEEDS OFFICE SUPPLIES, HAVE YOUR DUPLICATING DONE HERE, LETTERS TYPED, COPIED, DO YOU NEED A SECRETARY?

How incredible, she thought. She never would have noticed a shop like this if she hadn't been looking.

Julie was still glued to the other window and Nancy stood still. Now was the moment. Were they going in – or not? Was it a risky thing to do? She knew Bob's thoughts. There was no one in either shop ... perhaps they should forget it? At that moment, though, a man emerged from the office and came towards them. He carried his hat in his hand; maybe he was going to lunch? He was a well-dressed man of middle height, balding, but with a good carriage, upright as a ramrod. Nancy guessed immediately – ex-army.

His eyes were brown, warm and kindly, as he came towards them. 'Can I help you?'

'Well—' Nancy began, and thought, in for a penny ...

'Do come in,' he held out his hand. 'I'm John Leeds.'

She took his outstretched hand. 'Mrs Halliwell, and this is my daughter, Julie.'

Julie, who couldn't have appeared more sulky if she had tried, looked anywhere but at him.

'Is there something I can do for you?'

'Well—' she hesitated. 'I've really come about the advertisement in Lytton's window ...'

He looked so delighted that he put down his hat and rubbed his hands. 'Oh, this is wonderful! My first reply and I put it in four shops! Do come through, Mrs Halliwell.'

Julie stood her ground.

'This way,' he said, ignoring her obvious reluctance, and through the open doorway they went, to find themselves in a 'proper office', as Nancy later told Bob.

18

'Please sit down.' Nancy looked around curiously while Julie was unable to contain a shudder. All those files and boxes and machines. She felt slightly sick. If she didn't watch out her mother would land her in this mess.

'Now, perhaps I should explain the position,' he said.

'Please,' Nancy said, urging Julie with her eyes to be a little more attentive.

'As you can see, this is a shop in two parts; I bought it when I retired from the army. The idea was to carry on dealing with office supplies, which is a subject I know quite a lot about. I used to be in the city as a company director before the war.' He looked for approval at Julie, who turned away.

'I am sure you will understand, Mrs Halliwell, things have not been easy, especially at my age trying to find a job, so here I am. I stayed in the army after the war, and retired two years ago. Now my wife,' and Nancy heaved a great inward sigh of relief, 'carries – or rather I should say *did* carry – on the other part of the shop. Her parents died five years ago, and owned rather a lot of very nice furniture and antiques, and it was at her suggestion that we should open the other part and sell – or try to sell – antiques. It's not doing too badly as a matter of fact, but of course, my time is taken up, believe it or not, with the office side which is doing reasonably well. I have two sons, twelve and fourteen, far too young to help me.'

'And your wife?' Nancy said; she was beginning to get the picture.

'Unfortunately she has been ill for the last three months with arthritis and it isn't getting any better. She comes in less and less and I really don't want to close the shop down as it is doing quite well as a small source of income. We talked about it, Alice and I, and wondered

19

what the possibilities were of having someone to help. I cannot afford an assistant,' he smiled apologetically, 'so we came up with this idea: of someone helping in the shop when I am not here, or at lunch, or out seeing a customer in exchange for being taught general office routine, shorthand and typing.'

Nancy thought it a splendid idea, but by Julie's face knew it wasn't going to work.

He was looking at Julie politely, obviously waiting for her to say something.

'How old are you, Miss Halliwell?'

'Sixteen,' she said.

'And leaving school at Easter, I suppose?'

'Yes,' she said shortly.

'Which school do you attend?'

'The Central school.'

'So you will have done shorthand and typing to a degree?'

'Yes, but—'

'But?' he smiled at her, and looked so fatherly, that she blurted out, 'I don't want to do office work!'

'Julie!' Nancy cried, mortified.

'Well, it's true!'

'What did you want to do?'

'Anything but—' she said with a trace of her old humour.

'Well, I cannot force you to anything, the decision must be yours, but let me explain. Shorthand and typing are not all office work consists of; there are some other very interesting things, and you would be learning. It would not be like being at school with other girls – you might even find it enjoyable. Does the shop part of it interest you?'

Despite herself, Julie said, 'Yes, I think I'd like that,

but not at the expense of doing shorthand and typing.'

Mr Leeds looked compassionately at Nancy as though they shared a problem together. 'What do you think, Mrs Halliwell?'

'I think it's a good idea; she could train and at the same time get experience of a shop; she might not like it.'

'Well, I suggest you go home and talk it over. I could only pay five shillings a week pocket-money but she would be receiving tuition free of charge.'

'Of course,' Nancy said, embarrassed.

'In the meantime I will wait and see if I have any more replies; are you on the telephone?'

'No,' Nancy said.

'Well, let me give you a few days to think about it, and perhaps you will let me know.'

'Thank you,' Nancy said, and now that she was leaving Julie gave him one of her rare smiles.

'Thank you, Mr Leeds.'

As they left the shop, he looked after them. Well, it didn't look too hopeful, but he had only had one reply; there might be others . . .

'I've never felt so embarrassed in my life!' Julie cried, hurrying on.

'Well, I didn't know where to put my face when he asked us in. It's done now and you must admit, Julie, it is an opportunity for someone – even if it's not you.'

'Yes,' Julie said grudgingly, 'I can see the point of it. If it were not for the office part, I'd quite like to work in that other little shop.'

'Well, there's no future there, my girl,' Nancy said sternly. 'I thought he was such a nice man.'

'He was, but that's not the point. Let's cross over and go into the little café.'

By now, Julie was quite enjoying her little trip out. They found a table and ordered tea and scones, and Julie keenly watched the well-dressed people walking by; it was certainly a cut above Balmoral Street. She stared hard at smart housewives, baskets over their arms, mostly wearing hats and gloves – it was a nice area. Without giving anything away, Julie was actually milling over the possibilities. She couldn't get her mind off that little red antique chair and the pile of soft laces and linens, and the muslin-draped Moses basket. Still, that was not what it was all about. Imagine the rest of it, sitting in that dark office, with that Roneo or whatever it was, and the typewriters . . .

Nancy said nothing on the way home. The decision would have to be Julie's. As far as she was concerned, she saw it as a nice little stop-gap, an opportunity, learning how to do shorthand and typing properly, and to run an office, and he looked as if he would be very good at his job of teaching. The other part – the antique part – she gave little thought to. As far as she was concerned it was not important.

Nothing more was said, and when they reached home Julie went straight upstairs to her room, which was all hers now that Eileen had gone, and back to her beloved magazines.

She came downstairs once her father had come in, and he washed and combed his hair before sitting down to his dinner, which Nancy took out of the oven.

'So how did you get on then?' he asked. He could see by Nancy's face that there was no joy there.

'Well, it was interesting. Even Julie thought so. Of course, a *lovely* area, and a real office supplies shop and next door this sort of antique shop—'

'You mean a junk shop!' Bob exploded, putting his knife and fork down.

Even Julie tried to soothe him. 'No, Dad, not like that. Real antiques – you know, nice things, pretty things. His wife usually runs it but she is ill, so . . .'

'At least he has a wife, then,' Bob said, resuming his meal. 'What did you think, Julie?'

She laughed. 'Well, it was quite an interesting set-up – but not for me,' she said hastily. 'Same old bind – office work – but a chance for someone, I suppose.' And nothing more was said.

On Sunday morning she and Gwen went to church together in their best coats and hats, one tall and fair, the other small and dark-haired. Going into the village they came to the corner of Church Lane, and walked down the pathway to St Luke's church. The back pews were occupied by most of the boys and girls they knew from school, and a fair amount of note-passing and message-throwing was going on. Once the choir and the vicar arrived they rose to their feet and sang lustily.

'We never see Les Daly in church, do we?' whispered Gwen.

'He's probably a Catholic,' Julie answered. 'His mother's Irish.'

'Is there a Mr Daly?'

'No, Mrs Daly is a widow.'

'The merry widow,' Gwen giggled.

'Ssshhh—'

Afterwards they did their favourite thing, walking into the park before going home for Sunday lunch. They sat by the tennis courts watching the lucky young people playing on this glorious Sunday morning.

'I'd like to play tennis,' Gwen said.

'You'll be lucky,' Julie replied. 'Still, I'm not bothered; I'm not really the sporting type.'

'You don't have to be to like tennis,' Gwen said. 'My dad used to play.'

'Really?' Julie could hardly believe it. Parents, playing tennis? She tried to imagine her own father wielding a tennis racket.

Two young men came towards them swinging their rackets, with white trousers and pullovers draped around their shoulders. They were making for the seat in front of Julie and Gwen while they waited for a free court.

They sat down, turning round briefly to smile, and Julie's face was crimson. One of the boys was Les Daly. She thought she would die . . . so overcome, she made an effort to move. Only the high wire netting separated them!

But Gwen held on to her firmly. 'Don't go,' she whispered.

Les Daly turned round and stood up. 'Excuse me, but don't I know you?' He looked at both of them while the other boy smiled.

'I think I've seen you before.'

'We usually come here after church,' Gwen said. She was the more poised of the two, while Julie sat tongue-tied.

'Oh, I see. Do you play?'

'Tennis?' Gwen said. 'No,' as if it were by choice rather than something her parents couldn't afford.

'You live in Balmoral Street, don't you?' Les asked turning his handsome face to Julie. Oh, he was beautiful close to, she thought, even better-looking.

'Yes,' she gulped.

He smiled. 'I thought I'd seen you there.'

'Really?' She sounded genuinely surprised.

'Yes. My mother runs the off licence.'

'I say, this one's free,' the other boy said as a pair left the tennis court.

'Nice meeting you,' Les said. 'I'm Les Daly, by the way, and this is Martin Young.'

'And I am Gwen Edwards and this is my friend Julie Halliwell.'

'Nice to meet you. See you,' and they were gone.

Julie was almost quaking in her shoes. 'Oh, Gwen!'

'Yes, I have to say he is quite something,' Gwen said. 'Even better close to. The other one was nice, too.'

They watched the boys at play for a few minutes, then decided it was time they went home.

'Oh, what a day!' Julie said. 'My lucky day . . . except Eileen will be there when I get home.'

'You do realise it's Easter next week and we break up on Tuesday.'

'Our last day – I can't wait!' Julie said.

It came round at last, leaving day, and the two friends walked home together for the last time without a backward glance.

'Shall we go up to the fair on Bank Holiday?' Julie asked.

Gwen was doubtful. 'I think I am going down to my gran's in Wales.'

'Oh, I wish I was going somewhere.'

'Also,' Gwen said slowly, 'I've got an interview when we get back.'

Julie stopped and turned. 'An interview. Where?'

'At the local council offices.'

Julie looked horrified. 'Gwen!'

'Well, it's a start.'

'Rather you than me,' she said. It quite clouded her leaving as she realized that no longer would they be together, going to school every day; and whatever she did herself, it would not be near Gwen. 'Council offices – how dreary!'

*

25

Gwen went to Wales and Bob and Nancy and Julie went up to the fair on Easter Monday. On Friday Gwen had her interview. It was a foregone conclusion that she would get through it, and she came round in the evening to tell Julie all about it.

'Oh, Mrs Halliwell! It's so exciting – beautiful offices and I shall be in the planning department. I start on Monday.'

'Did you have to take tests?'

'Oh, yes,' Gwen said proudly. 'Typing and short-hand.'

'Well, you're good at them,' Julie said, just a little sourly.

'I happen to like them,' Gwen said. 'Smashing type-writers – modern – not like those at school.'

How could typewriters be smashing? Julie thought.

'I expect your mum and dad are pleased,' Nancy Halliwell said, with a sidelong glance at Julie. She wondered just how Julie would take it. Their lives would be so different from now on.

'And you won't have far to go.'

'No, I can walk, or it's a tuppenny tram ride.'

'Come on upstairs to my room,' Julie said. 'I want to show you something. There's a new *Picture Play* out and Mum let me buy it for Easter.'

On Saturday morning a typewritten letter arrived for Mrs Halliwell – a rare occurrence in that house. She read it carefully:

Dear Mrs Halliwell,

I am wondering what you finally decided about Julie's future. I had one other reply and the girl is willing to start, but I have to say I thought your daughter would be the more suitable of the two.

I wouldn't wish to put pressure on you but would like to know if you have come to a decision.

Yours faithfully,
John L. Leeds

Her cheeks flaming with embarrassment, Nancy read the letter three times. She really should have let him know before this, but truth to tell had been secretly hoping that Julie would change her mind. Well, she would have to write and tell him; it was definitely not for Julie.

When Julie, who had walked up to the library in order to pass Les Daly's shop in the hope of seeing him, came in, the letter was on the mantelpiece.

She eyed it curiously. 'Blackheath – who's it from?'

'Mr Leeds,' Nancy said nonchalantly. 'You can read it.'

Julie read it through once, then again, and Nancy noticed that her cheeks were flushed.

'We should have let him know before,' she said as if the blame were hers.

'Yes, we should.'

'Still,' Julie said, 'He will be pleased to know that I've thought it over and decided to give it a try.'

'Julie!'

Nancy's eyes were wide as she stared at her daughter in disbelief.

'Well, why not?' Julie said, and her eyes were mischievous, 'I don't have to stay if I don't like it.'

'Oh, but Julie—'

'You will have to make it all right with Dad though—' but Nancy was already in the hall putting on her coat.

'What are you doing?'

'We're going over to Mr Leeds to tell him. There's no

27

time like the present, he's waited long enough already. It's quicker than the post.'

Julie, excited now, eyed herself in the mirror and went upstairs to put her best coat on. Now that she had decided the die was cast. As she said, she didn't have to stay if she didn't like it.

In any case, Nancy thought, they couldn't afford to keep her there long with no money coming in, although it was easier now that Eileen had left home. But then that was the whole point; if she was well trained she should be able to get a good job.

She couldn't believe she was going to see that nice Mr Leeds again . . .

Chapter Three

As they neared the shop, Nancy's heart began to beat
faster, but Julie waked tall beside her as if she hadn't a
care in the world. The door was closed today, but Nancy
pushed it open and there was Mr Leeds in the inside
office poring over some papers. He came forward swiftly
to greet them; it was easy to see the hopeful expression
on his face.

'Well, good morning, Mrs Halliwell, Miss Halliwell –
have you some good news for me?' He beamed at them.
'Take a seat, please.'

'Good morning, Mr Leeds, I must apologize for
keeping you waiting so long, but we have given it a lot of
hard thought, and Julie has decided that she would like to
take advantage of the position you are offering.' Nancy
looked encouragingly at Julie.

Mr Leeds rubbed his hands together. 'Well, I am
pleased, and I hope you will be too, after my tuition,'
he smiled. The door opened and a couple came in.
'Excuse me, please,' then, as he disappeared through
the door, he added, 'make yourselves comfortable. I
shouldn't be long.'

It seemed that the couple were interested in a particular plate. He wrapped it carefully and gave it to them,

brought the money back into the till, then sat down again.

'My wife would normally be here, on a Saturday morning especially.'

'Would Julie be expected to work on Saturdays?' Nancy asked.

'Well, Saturday morning gets quite busy, and it's usually a busy time in the office too. We close at one on Saturday; all the shops on this parade do.'

'I see.'

'Does that worry you?' he asked Julie.

'No, not at all,' she replied. In fact now that she was here she was getting excited and trying not to think about the office bit.

He sat down at his desk. 'Well, now, what more can I tell you? The hours are from nine until five, nine-thirty till one on Saturday. How far away do you live?'

'In Balmoral Street,' Julie said. 'That's—'

'Yes, I know it. Well, I expect you will want to bring sandwiches for your lunch. I usually go home since I live just round the corner, and your coming will allow me to leave the shop open during the lunch hour so you will be in charge, young lady. But not yet awhile,' as he saw Nancy's air of consternation. 'We'll wait until you get used to it.'

His kind brown eyes rested on Julie. 'I thought it might be a good idea if we gave it a month's trial; that way if you don't like it you can tell me. Also, of course, you may not suit me,' and he smiled. 'But I have every hope . . . When could you start? Next Monday?'

Julie looked at her mother, and Nancy nodded. 'Yes, that would be suitable.'

'Very well,' and he got up, and shook hands with them. 'I will explain your duties more clearly to you on

30

Monday. I look forward to seeing you then.'

'Good morning, Mr Leeds.'

They left the shop and made straight for the little café. They ordered coffee. Nancy was surprised to see that Julie even looked a little excited. She prayed that it would work. It might turn out to be the best thing . . .

On Monday Julie was ready early. She brushed her thick fair hair until it shone and put on her navy skirt, a white blouse and her navy reefer coat. Nancy had given her a navy leather handbag, and she carried a small packet of sandwiches and an apple her mother had insisted on her taking.

On her way to the shop Julie cast a quick glance over at the off licence, but of course it was always closed in the mornings. She walked on until she came to the top road, and feeling quite important she made her way along the Old Dover Road. She was five minutes early. Mr Leeds was already there; he had had no doubt that she would turn up; they were not the sort of people to let a man down, he had surmised. And there she was. He hoped for her sake she would settle down as much as for his.

'Good morning. May I call you Julie?' he asked.

'Of course,' she said.

'Now go through the inner office and you will find a little kitchen and a cloakroom. There is a toilet and somewhere to hang your clothes – and a wash basin. When you are ready come back to the office.'

A small desk and chair had been put in front of the window. On it sat a typewriter, a block of paper and a shorthand notebook, which Julie eyed with misgivings.

'I want you to get as much typing practice as you can,' he said. 'Only practice can make your speed any good, and of course accurate. We must do at least an hour's shorthand practice every day,' and he ignored the look of distaste on her face. 'First of all I would like you to copy this letter exactly as it is so that I can see how far you have got in typing. I will leave you with that for the moment.'

Julie inserted the paper in the machine and got to work. Laboriously she got through the letter without too many mistakes.

'Speed is not what we're aiming for, accuracy is more important. There's quite a lot of work involved to erase your mistakes.'

I wish I hadn't come, Julie thought dismally. I hate it, I hate all of it; and then the door opened and he hurried forth to help a woman with a walking stick. He kissed her and led her to a chair in the outer office.

'Come through, Julie,' he called, and she dutifully left the typewriter.

The woman was pretty, or had been, but now her face was creased with pain, as she settled herself carefully in a chair. 'My wife,' he explained to Julie, who decided the woman had come to check her over – that she wouldn't be a menace to her still handsome husband.

'Hallo, Mrs Leeds,' she said, holding out her hand. 'I'm feeling very nervous, I'm afraid.'

'I'm not surprised,' Mrs Leeds said, 'your first day after leaving school. But he isn't an ogre, you'll find – he is really quite kind. I'm just so sorry I can't be here; I loved being in the little shop. But there, we never know what's going to happen in the future, do we? And as you see I am not as mobile as I used to be.'

'I'm sorry—' Julie began.

'How do you feel about the antiques – do you know anything about them?'

'No,' Julie replied, her blue eyes coming to life. 'But I

32

am very keen to learn.'

'Yes, it is a fascinating subject. We have lots of books at home if you are interested; my husband can bring some down.'

'Time enough for that,' Mr Leeds said. 'This young lady has to learn how to run an office. She is typing her first letter for me.'

'Oh, then I mustn't interrupt.'

Her kind blue eyes met Julie's. 'I hope you enjoy it; you will, you know, after a time, and I know my husband is relieved to have some help.'

'Thank you,' Julie said, and went back to her machine. What a nice woman . . .

Julie was surprised how many customers came in with orders for the office. Mr Leeds was kept on his feet for most of the morning, special kinds of paper, carbons, labels, typewriter ribbons, folders, orders for copies on the Roneo – and one lady asking the price of the chair . . .

At lunch time, she looked up from her typing. He was quite right, if she didn't rush she became more accurate. Though she was sick of copying and felt hungry, the morning had flown by.

'I'll close the shop at lunch time for this week. Next week perhaps we'll stay open; it depends how you feel. In the meantime, I'm off to lunch, so make yourself some tea or coffee – there's a kettle and a gas ring in the kitchen – and make yourself acquainted with the premises.'

He turned the notice round to CLOSED and the key in the lock.

Julie made herself a pot of tea and, feeling very important to be in charge, sat at her desk eating her sandwiches. She would save the apple and eat it going home.

She couldn't wait to go inside the smaller shop and look at all the things and the price tabs on them. She was fascinated; imagine owing them all – Mrs Leeds' parents must have had a lovely home . . .

She walked round the office looking at all the shelves and what they contained and decided they must be the most boring things ever. Still, she must make the best of it; there was the other side of it, and he was such a nice man, she would hate to let him down. When he returned from lunch he gave her some filing to do.

'All these files are in alphabetical order: this one A–D, the next one E–G and so on. I'd like you to file this bundle of letters in this cabinet, the latest date in the front. A well-run filing system is the answer to an efficient office,' he said.

Julie found she quite enjoyed doing this; it appealed to her sense of order. She filed the last letter with the satis-faction of a job well done.

After that she was asked to tidy the shelves and make a note of what they contained and finally at the end of the day he dictated a letter to her in shorthand.

'Can you read it back?' he asked.

'I think so.'

'Then type it out – and don't worry, it's only a prac-tice letter.'

She was surprised how busy he was kept in the shop, with people coming in for stationery and orders for copies.

'Later on in the week, I'll show you how to copy on the duplicator,' he said and her heart sank. The look of the big drum-shaped thing was enough to put her off.

Just before five o'clock he was busy with a customer

when a woman came in to the antiques section and wished to see a particular dish.

He beckoned Julie from the office. 'Just see what the customer wants, will you. I'll be with you in a moment.'

'Good afternoon,' Julie said, her heart thumping.

'Oh, hello,' the woman said. 'I was looking at the dish, the green one. Could I see it?'

Julie lifted it off the shelf gingerly and held it out to her.

'Oh, it's lovely,' she said, fingering it. 'How much is it?'

Julie turned it over, where the label read seven and six.

The woman looked doubtful, and Julie was relieved then to find Mr Leeds at her side, smiling.

'Majolica,' he said.

She nodded. 'Yes, I collect it – oh, but I must have it.'

'It's a very nice piece,' Mr Leeds said, taking it from her and going towards the till.

'You'll find some tissue paper underneath the counter, Julie,' he said. 'Wrap it carefully.' He rang up the money.

'I have a bag,' the woman said, 'then it can go in my basket.'

'Thank you, Madam,' Mr Leeds said, and turned to Julie. 'Well, you've just made your first sale. And now young lady, it's almost five o'clock – time you went home. Put the cover on your machine.'

'Thank you, Mr Leeds.'

'I'll see you tomorrow.'

Julie walked home on air.

On Sunday she and Gwen walked to church telling each other of their experiences.

'You could have knocked me down with a feather when you told me what you were doing. I thought you didn't want office work?'

'I didn't – but you know what my mum is like, and it's an odd set-up – part of it is an antique shop,' she explained to Gwen, who frowned.

'Sounds funny to me. Did your dad go along with it?'

'My mum persuaded him. And what about you? How about the council offices?'

'Oh, it's great – ever so busy and one or two people we know from school – Jimmy Dale . . .'

'Oh, him,' Julie said scathingly, but by now they were at the church. Once inside they sang as lustily as ever.

'Shall we go into the park?' Gwen asked after the service, with a sidelong glance at her friend.

'Why not?' Julie replied casually, and they made their way to the tennis courts. There, already playing, were Les Daly and Martin Young.

'Don't let's sit too near,' Julie said.

'It's the only vacant seat,' replied Gwen.

They watched the boys play, and after a time, Julie said, 'I could sit here all day watching them.'

'So could I,' Gwen said. 'I quite like Martin.'

Once, noticing them, Les waved and Julie blushed and waved back.

The game went on, then presently, Julie got up. 'Come on, Gwen, we'll be late home if we don't go now.'

Grudgingly they set off home, talking non-stop.

'See you tomorrow night,' Gwen said.

As the days wore on and spring turned into summer, Julie found that she was enjoying her job more than she had ever thought possible. Being in charge during the lunch hour was the first joy, and selling her first few items; even the shorthand and typing, she found, weren't as bad the more you got used to them. It was nothing like school with them all going at once. She was able to take letters now quite easily and even took her shorthand instruction book home with her sometimes, much to Nancy's surprise. Mr Leeds was a mine of information about running an office and gave her lots of useful hints.

'If you are asked to do something, say you can do it,' he told her, 'and if you can't – learn afterwards. Don't admit to a lack of knowledge. Nothing is beyond you if you try.' He was like a second father to her.

As for Mrs Leeds, she came in whenever she could, armed with books on antiques. Sometimes a delivery van would come and deposit another piece of furniture or some more china. Julie found herself with an absorbing, growing interest. She would browse round the shops, especially looking at the antique shops in Blackheath on her way home, finding what she liked most and trying to assess its value. Her ambition now was to learn more about the antique trade itself and see if she could find a job, perhaps in London at one of the large antique houses or auctioneers.

But behind it all lay the threat of war. There was talk of it the whole summer, children and those mothers-to-be who wished to go had been evacuated to what was hoped to be places of safety in the event of war; there was even talk of Bob's factory being moved up north to a safer area. They knew in London they would be targeted if all the rumours that were rife came to pass.

Nancy would have none of it. All talk, she said – but it was to cover her fear. Eileen, home sometimes at the weekend, was almost certain that war was coming, and suggested that they should move away to a place of safety.

'But what about your father?' Nancy demanded. 'We couldn't leave him behind.'

In August Julie was given two weeks' holiday, and she and Nancy went down to Devon to stay with Nancy's mother, who saw little enough of her daughter. Julie had her seventeenth birthday down there and her father came down for the weekend. They all went back on the train together. It was then that Bob told Nancy that it was almost definite that the factory was being moved to Yorkshire, in the depths of the country; they were converting an old woollen mill and making homes up there for the families from London.

Nancy was horrified. She didn't know whether to believe Bob or not. But with the dawn of September what they feared most came to pass.

England was at war. The life of everyone would change and never be the same again.

It was at the end of October that Bob was finally sent up to Yorkshire on his own; the wives and families could if they wished follow later when the emergency dwellings would be ready. Apart from a few false air-raid warnings, everyone was just thankful that the raids had not started; some thought they never would. Sandbags filled the streets, corrugated iron shelters were erected in gardens and on open land, building began on underground brick shelters; but the black-out was the hardest thing to contend with.

Eileen came home one weekend to announce that she had got herself a small flat in Notting Hill. It was cheap and convenient. Her staff was being distributed all over London for the time being, and her office would be in Kensington. In the event of really bad raids their offices would be moved down into the country. Julie was envious – trust Eileen to fall on her feet.

In the meantime, Julie continued working for John Leeds. She had now become quite adept at shorthand and typing, and loved keeping everything in order. Mr Leeds put her on to the day books and ledgers because she was so neat and thorough and, what was more, she discovered she enjoyed it. She scrupulously kept track of stock, making notes and becoming more confident every day. Most of all she loved it when customers came into the antique shop. Most of them by now wanted to sell rather than buy, and there was a limit as to how much the shop would take. Sometimes Mrs Leeds would come down and join her for lunch, bringing antique books for her to browse through. That was the part she enjoyed most.

By Christmas she had quite settled in. John Leeds was surprised how efficient she was, and thought she probably didn't realize it herself. She was quick to point out when bills were not paid. He tended to be a little tardy on the matter himself – his wife had always kept him up to date – and she checked when they were running out of stock. Everything was so neat and tidy it was a joy to open up in the morning. She started her day with dusting every piece on its shelf, and now and again polish if she had time, then seeing that everything was to hand for Mr Leeds; he had never been so well looked after. And this was the girl who told him once that she had wanted to be an actress! She even learned how to run the duplicating machine and was surprised by how, in the end, everything was so simple.

Christmas was fairly quiet that year; everyone seemed to be waiting for something to happen. The streets were full of soldiers, sailors and airmen on leave and the displays were pathetic, most of the windows being stuck with strips of paper against bomb blast. People faced the New Year with misgivings. Rumours abounded. When would this phoney war end? Bob came home, and reluctantly went back. He missed his family more than he thought possible, but admitted that the countryside was lovely and it was different again from London. The converted dwellings would be ready at any time, and he told Nancy to be prepared.

'Bob,' she said, worried. 'What will happen to Julie? She won't want to come with us.'

'She'll have to,' Bob replied. 'We can't let her stay down here on her own. Where would she live?'

That was true.

They heard in February that March was to be the date for moving families up north to be with their menfolk. Julie was near to tears. 'What will I do in Yorkshire?' she asked. 'I've only just got settled in this job.'

'It'll stand you in good stead, you'll see,' Nancy said wisely.

When she told Mr Leeds he was quite upset at the thought of losing her.

'I would like you to have seen the year out,' he said, 'say, until early summer. I am just wondering – you see, if the raids really start I will want to take my wife and the boys away from London. We have already discussed it.'

'I see.' So, Julie thought, if they do start I shall lose my job anyway.

'And always hoping of course things don't get worse, I was wondering if perhaps you could come and stay with us once your mother goes? I am sure my wife would be very glad to have you and we have plenty of room.'

Julie knew a moment of excitement. Oh, if only she could! Then thought how her mother would not go along with it.

'Look, I'll mention it tonight,' he said. 'What do you think?'

'Well, I would be very happy; I don't want to leave London, but I don't know what my mother would say.'

'Of course,' he said, 'I understand.'

Alice Leeds was more than agreeable. It would be nice to have someone young like Julie around the house, and it would only be a temporary situation. She missed the boys, they being at boarding school.

Julie broached the matter with her mother, who told her at once not to be silly. Nancy did however think about it, and came to the conclusion it might be a solution while they thought about what was going to happen to Julie once they had left London.

'You'd better see what Mrs Leeds has to say on the matter,' she said. 'Mind – I'm making no promises.' She wrote to Bob that night, and told him what had been suggested.

Rumours about the threatened air raids were rife, and Nancy became apprehensive.

John Leeds came in the morning to tell Julie that his wife had agreed, but as a temporary measure, because of course in the event of raids they would be moving away themselves and doubtless Julie would join her parents in Yorkshire.

Julie was over the moon, while Nancy suggested that she would like to meet Mrs Leeds – it was only right – they needed to know each other, and asked Julie to suggest to her employer that she should call on Mrs Leeds the next day.

So it was all arranged. In March, when the family moved

away from Balmoral Street, Julie would go to stay with the Leeds family. She couldn't wait to tell Gwen of their plans, and on Christmas Eve, their hats pulled down and their fur collars about their ears, they went to the library before it closed.

'What are you going to do if the raids start?' Julie asked.

Gwen shrugged. 'Don't know. No one's mentioned it – you know my dad, he keeps everything close to his chest.'

'Hmm.'

And then on the way back they bumped into Les Daly.

'Girls,' he said. 'I haven't seen you for ages – what have you been up to?'

Julie nearly swooned.

'We're both working,' Gwen said. 'I work at the council offices and Julie—'

Julie intervened. 'In an office in Blackheath,' she said.

'Oh, good-oh,' he said. 'Do you like it?'

'Yes, it's great,' Gwen said, while Julie couldn't take her eyes off him.

'Well,' he said. 'I'm off to the Navy.'

'What?' they said together.

'My father was in the Navy, so I'm doing the same thing. I go next week.'

Julie could have wept. Still, if she was moving away, she wouldn't see him anyway. But he might get killed – her beloved Les.

She held out her hand, her nervousness forgotten now. 'Good luck,' she said.

'Thanks,' he said, smiling at her. 'To both of you, too.'

And he was gone.

'Oh, I can't bear it!' Julie cried.

'Oh, come on, it's not as if you were married to him,' Gwen laughed.

'I wish I were,' Julie said, and as they huddled together to keep out the cold, they hurried home.

Chapter Four

Julie hurried home as fast as her legs could carry her. Today was the day her mother had gone to see Mrs Leeds, and she couldn't wait to see her reaction. If only . . .

She pushed open the door and almost ran down the narrow hall.

'Well,' Nancy said, her floury hands in the mixing bowl. 'I hope you are not going to get carried away with all that luxury living.'

'Mum!' Julie cried. 'You mean – you saw Mrs Leeds – what did she say? What do you think?'

'Calm down,' Nancy said. 'Just let me get this pastry on to the board.'

Julie's shining eyes hardly left Nancy's face, as Nancy settled the pastry on the board and rinsed her hands.

'Well,' she said. 'You are a very lucky girl, I must say. She's a lovely woman, Mrs Leeds.'

'So I can go?' Julie cried.

'We couldn't refuse an offer like that. But you must behave yourself, my girl. I only wish I had had the opportunity to live in such a house.'

'Why?' Julie was puzzled.

'It is the most beautiful house I have ever seen,' Nancy

said. 'It is enormous, a great Victorian house, filled with lovely things – furniture – ornaments; it belonged to Mrs Leeds' parents, and when they died it was left to her as the only child. I think Mr Leeds did very well for himself – but he's a nice man, I'll say that for him. So that's what they are doing, selling off the stuff in the shop, more's the pity. Still, as she said, with a war on, you never know. They might move away if the raids start. It doesn't bear thinking of . . .'

'Oh, thank you, Mum.' Julie was so grateful, she wanted to throw her arms around her mother's neck, but being demonstrative was not usual in that house. Nancy was a good and loving mother, but seldom, if ever, petted the girls.

'So when do I go?' she asked. She could hardly wait.

'As soon as I go up and join your father in a couple of weeks. Of course, it's only a temporary measure; if the raids start, they'll be off and so will you. You'll have to come up to us.'

Julie's face dropped. Oh, please don't let the raids start.

The war was hotting up in France although Nancy didn't get away until the beginning of April, and by that time half the rooms in Balmoral Street were empty where families from the factory had been evacuated. Exhorting Julie to be careful and to come home at the first sign of trouble, Nancy was almost tearful when she said goodbye. Julie, her luggage packed, arrived at the Leeds' front door not knowing if she were coming or going.

She was surprised at how upset she had been to see her mother go, but at the sight of Mr and Mrs Leeds to welcome her, she felt a sense of relief. She was so over-come by the opulence of the house, never dreaming it would be as grand as it was, that it helped to take away her sorrow at her mother's leaving. She had never stayed away from home before.

She was shown to a bedroom on the first floor, a room filled with fine French furniture with its own little dressing room. The house had seven bedrooms and was on three floors and Julie was quite overcome. Her feet sinking into thick rugs on polished floors, surrounded by dark paintings, she unpacked her few things and made her way downstairs. The great chandelier in the hall was lit, casting a glow over everything, while heavy dark curtains swathed the windows to keep out the light. She smiled as she thought of her mother's black sateen lining – the answer of most of Balmoral Street to the blackout problem.

The kitchen was enormous and old-fashioned with heavy wooden furniture, scrubbed almost white. She doubted whether the great larders, for use in much more affluent days, were full.

'I brought my ration book,' she smiled. 'Mum reminded me.'

'Oh, good,' Mrs Leeds said. 'And your gas mask, I hope. God forbid! We have supper ready this evening – I have a very good help – Mrs Norton. She comes in daily to give me a hand, but how much longer she will stay is anybody's guess. She'll want to do more for the war effort I expect.'

Julie felt completely at home. After supper, they listened to the radio while Mr Leeds went into his study to work. Julie went to bed early, feeling that she couldn't wait to sink into that wonderful bed with its feather-filled eiderdown. She thought of her parents and what they were doing up there in Yorkshire, and was pleased that her mother had joined her father at last. As for herself, she wished this life could go on. In the morning, she would get up and go with Mr Leeds to the office which was within walking distance.

The day after Nancy moved up to Yorkshire, the first British civilian was killed in an air raid on the Orkneys, and this was enough to put everyone on alert. The news from France began to filter in. The Germans had invaded Denmark and Norway, The Netherlands and Luxembourg so that by the beginning of May when they invaded France and made great headway it was fairly obvious that England would be next. The British troops had their backs to the wall, and the rush to get them home was on.

Those few days building up to Dunkirk were some of the worst of the war. John Leeds appeared to be very worried, and he and Alice Leeds spent long hours talking and making plans. Julie had the freedom to look over the house at all the lovely things, and the more she saw of such beauty, the more enraptured she became. She couldn't bear to think her time was limited, that she might have to leave it all and join her mother and father in Yorkshire. But she mustn't think about it. There were several raid alerts and the three of them went down into the cellar where it was freezing cold but reputedly safer than staying upstairs in the house. When everything was quiet, Julie helped Mrs Leeds with the housework, dusting all the precious articles, being as useful as she could to an already partly crippled woman.

One Saturday afternoon in late May, Julie made her way back to Balmoral Street. The plane trees were in pale green leaf, but there was an air of dereliction about everything. Windows boarded up, or criss-crossed with

brown sticky tape, sandbags outside the off licence shop
... Julie shivered and made her way to Gwen's.

'I'm glad you've come,' Gwen said. 'I thought we'd
go to the library and have a walk in the park. OK?'

'Yes, sure,' Julie said. 'How's everything with you?'

'I'll tell you on the way,' said Gwen, soon linking
arms with Julie like old times.

'My mum is going down to Devon with my little
brother. Dad says it's going to get very nasty – and he
should know,' she grinned.

'Really? But what about you?'

'I'm staying here to look after him, although he says if
it gets really bad I shall have to go with Mum – but I
don't want to. I'd rather stay in London, raids or no
raids. He can't go, you see, he is needed here. He has
rather an important position.' She was very proud of her
father. 'What about you? How are you getting on with
the Leeds?'

'Oh, it's great,' Julie said. 'Such a wonderful house,
and they are so nice. Although to tell you the truth I
don't know how much longer it can last. I have a feeling
they will be moving away soon. Mr Leeds won't want to
stay and keep that business going if it gets any worse.'

'You don't really think you'll have to go up to
Yorkshire, do you? It's dead up there.'

'I know,' and Julie made a face. 'Dad says the countryside is beautiful, but of course, there's nothing to do.'

Gwen grimaced. 'Poor you,' she said. She stole a sidelong glance at her friend.

'Les Daly's gone. He's based in Portsmouth. His
mother told my dad ...'

But Julie made no reply.

On Sunday morning after breakfast, Mr Leeds asked
Julie to join him and his wife in the drawing room where

they had something to tell her. Her heart sank – she knew what was coming, that they had decided to leave. And who could blame them? With the odd raider getting through the anti-aircraft guns and barrage balloons and the air-raid sirens shrieking day and night, who knew when the Luftwaffe would really be here. It didn't bear thinking of.

'I'm sorry about this, Julie my dear,' Mrs Leeds said, taking her hand. 'You've been a good girl to us – but of course we did know it would only be temporary didn't we?'

Julie nodded.

Mr Leeds cleared his throat. 'My wife and I have talked about this for quite some time, and I think we already knew that we would leave some day. I personally believe that the raids will come, and very soon, and we have already planned to move down to Cornwall and take the boys with us. That means closing the shop and getting rid of all this stuff—' he looked around. 'I don't need to tell you how much damage a bomb would make on this furniture – it is worth a great deal of money. Our future, in fact.

'So, Julie, we are going to sell most of it, but we shall take a few pieces with us. It was never our idea to live in such a grand style; we shall buy something small and comfortable – a cottage by the sea,' he smiled. 'But the rest of it we shall try to sell back to the dealers it was bought from and the rest put up for auction, as soon as possible, before the market gets overcrowded with unwanted stuff, so I am going to need your help.'

Sad though Julie felt at coming to the end of her stay, she was only too anxious to help in whatever way she could.

'From tomorrow, I would like you to go round every

49

room and catalogue everything that is in it. We shall go through when you have finished and pick out the things we intend to take.'

Julie felt miserable at the thought of it.

'When that's done we shall sort out the most valuable of the pieces and get in touch with the original galleries. Fortunately everything is well documented; Mr Leadbetter – my wife's father – kept excellent records. The not so important pieces can go to auction and we shall have a sale in the shop at the weekend. You can help me with that.'

Julie felt wretched; it had all come to an end too soon. She had known it was only a limited arrangement, but still – and she would have to write to her mother and tell her what was happening. Yorkshire! She couldn't bear the thought. But her face brightened at the thought of the task confronting her – she enjoyed a challenge.

'I shall put the shop in the agent's hands. Someone might be interested; an office supplies shop still has its uses, even in wartime, I did my bit last time, and now I'm too old to fight. We will have to adjust,' and he smiled across at his wife.

'We'll manage,' she said, confidently.

On Monday, Julie did not go to the office as usual, but armed with a large notebook and pen started on the top floor and worked her way down. It was incredible what the house contained, the collections of a lifetime, everything from china and glass to silver, well wrapped up in blue cloth and hidden in cupboards, to furniture the like of which Julie had never seen before. She had only reached half the first floor by lunchtime, when she joined Mrs Leeds in the kitchen.

'And what will you do?' Mrs Leeds asked kindly. 'Go

up to your parents as you arranged? You'll get used to it, Julie, Yorkshire is a lovely place.'

'But I think they're buried in the country somewhere, I can't imagine what I will do for a job.'

'Well, you could always join the Forces,' Mrs Leeds said, buttering her bread. 'I was in the WAAC in the First World War, that's where I met my husband.'

'Really?' Julie was fascinated.

'Yes, I loved it. I travelled all over, drove an ambulance. Here,' and from a drawer she brought out a snapshot of a pretty girl with a peaked cap in army uniform.

Julie smiled. 'Oh, that's lovely! How young you look, and the uniform suits you.'

'I think uniform suits everyone – there's something about it. Oh, yes I had a wonderful time.'

'I can't imagine my doing that, though,' Julie said slowly.

'No, perhaps not, but there are the WAAF, the ATS and the Wrens of course.'

But Julie couldn't imagine it. The discipline, the regimentation – she felt she was too much of a free spirit.

After a pot of tea, Julie went back to work and by the time Mr Leeds came home at six o'clock, she had got down to the ground floor.

'Good Lord,' he said glancing through the notebook. 'I never realized how much stuff we had. Tomorrow we will get all the bills and receipts out of the study and I'll show you what to do.'

The rest of that week was spent at the house, collating all the bills and receipts and the corresponding item, then the china with its bills, and the lamps. Everything was documented, which made Julie's job easier.

'Some of this furniture is what we call important,' Mr

Leeds told her, 'so I dare say the dealer will be prepared to buy it back. I hope so,' he added grimly, 'otherwise we shall lose a great deal of money. We shall have to store it in a safe place – it could get very complicated—'

Julie was made to file all the bills by name of supplier, and then date order, and when she had finished Mr Leeds got on the telephone to the original suppliers.

On Saturday she went into the shop. They put a large red SALE notice across the window and waited for people to arrive.

'We shall keep it going all next week at least. Depends how it goes,' Mr Leeds said.

The bargains seemed too good to miss for some people and the little shop became very busy. The takings soon mounted up and by the end of the day Julie was exhausted and longed for that lovely soft bed.

That same Saturday morning a letter came from Nancy telling Julie that she must come home to Yorkshire as soon as the Leeds left. It wasn't a bad place, she said, more conveniences than they had had in London – even a bathroom, and plenty of hot water. Each place had its small garden, Julie would love it. She and Julie's dad would be so pleased to see her again. Eileen had been up to see them and greatly approved.

She would, Julie thought darkly.

After that, things happened with great rapidity. The estate agent brought round an elderly widower who was interested in the shop; he had retired from his own business some two years before and missed it.

On Tuesday evening, a Mr de Gruyt was coming to dinner. He was the son of the original owner of the House of de Gruyt, a famous art and antique gallery. The elder Maurice de Gruyt was a Dutchman and a friend of

Mrs Leeds' father, who had bought a great deal of stock from him. Whenever Mr de Gruyt found something very special, he had always telephoned Mr Leadbetter first, who hurried up to London to see it. He had been an avid collector and at that time had plenty of money to pay for treasures, alas, losing most of it during the Depression.

The elder Mr de Gruyt was dead now, but this was his son, also Maurice, who still carried on the business.

'Let's hope he is prepared to buy some of the stuff back and give us a good price,' Mr Leeds said. 'Investing in antiques is a wonderful thing to do, but of course, it is chancy. Always a gamble, tastes change, and wars happen, but a really good piece never loses its value.'

Julie was fascinated. What a wonderful world she had found herself in.

So on Tuesday evening she hurried home to give Mrs Leeds some help in the kitchen. She laid the table in the almost unused dining room; they usually ate in the large kitchen-cum-breakfast room. Mrs Leeds asked her to put out all the fine china plates and the silver, cut-glass tumblers and wineglasses and a few roses on the table. The meal was to be soup followed by roast lamb and vegetables from the garden with a sweet to follow. Julie thought she had never seen anything quite so impressive in her life as the dining room with table laid.

Maurice de Gruyt turned out to be a fair-haired man, not young, or so Julie thought – twenty-nine, perhaps thirty – with a light complexion and very blue eyes of a startling clarity. Tall and good-looking – Julie was intrigued; she had never met a Dutchman before, and was slightly disappointed that he had no accent, but as Mr Leeds explained, he had been born and educated in this country.

Julie was asked to join them as they sat in the drawing room for drinks. Strange small glasses filled with yellow liquid were handed round, but Julie kept on the safe side and had orange juice. She had never tasted alcoholic liquor in her life.

She was introduced as Mr Leeds' secretary, a junior assistant who helped him in the shop and was learning all she could about the antique trade.

'She keeps the books; I don't know what I am going to do without her,' smiled Mr Leeds.

'You enjoy the work?' Maurice de Gruyt asked her.

'Yes, I love it, although I'm new to it.'

'It is another world,' he said.

Mrs Norton had offered to come in and serve the meal, which she did, afterwards doing the washing up. It was then that Mr de Gruyt and Mr Leeds disappeared, for they wanted to go round the house. Armed with Julie's notebook, they left, while Mrs Leeds stayed in the drawing room with Julie.

'Have you heard from your mother?' Mrs Leeds asked.

'Yes, she says the moment you leave I will have to take a train to Yorkshire,' and she looked so down that Mrs Leeds laughed.

'Oh, it won't be that bad, Julie,' she said. 'There are always compensations, and you will be with your family again.'

How to explain, Julie wondered, that she considered this elegance more her world than her parents' impoverished existence and felt guilty at the thought. She adored her father, thought him the best father in the world. But this new life had opened her eyes. Not used to it, she had gasped with open-eyed wonder at some of the things she had seen in this house. She knew them by name now,

54

having read the descriptions on the bills and receipts. Buhle cabinets, early seventeenth-century tables, delicate Venetian and Lalique glass, commodes, buttoned love seats, tulipwood chairs – there was no end to it. She knew it would take a lifetime to learn about it, but she couldn't imagine anything she would rather do and she longed to know more. And now that she would have to leave it all she couldn't have been more miserable.

When Mr de Gruyt and Mr Leeds returned it was late, and labels had been put on most of the things Mr de Gruyt would buy back. He left saying he would pay them another visit early the following week.

'Well, there we are. I knew he'd be pleased to get some of the pieces back and he's quoting good prices, considering.'

'What will he do with it all? How safe will it be?' asked Mrs Leeds.

'Oh, he has a special safe place for storage, and it won't be anywhere near London, you can rest assured of that.'

He smiled at Julie. 'Well, my dear, you did a good job of cataloguing; you must get to bed now. It's another day tomorrow.'

The week that followed was busy with other dealers coming down to inspect; Sotheby's, Christie's and other famous houses – while Julie was kept busy in the shop.

Mr de Gruyt stayed for lunch one day and she joined them.

'And what will you do with yourself, Julie?' he asked. 'You will miss working here, I expect.'

'Oh, yes, I will, I've loved it,' Julie said. 'My parents have been evacuated to Yorkshire, so I shall have to join them.'

'You will find quite a difference up there,' he smiled. 'Are you looking forward to it?'

'Not at all,' Julie grinned.

He and Mr Leeds disappeared into the study for a further conference, and when they came out, Mr de Gruyt prepared to leave, and Mr Leeds called Julie to come into the hall.

'I don't know what you will think of this, Julie,' he said. 'Mr de Gruyt was telling me he has lost his junior assistant to the RAF; a young man, and he wondered if you would be interested in taking over the job. What do you think? You don't have to answer now.'

'Oh!' her eyes were sparkling. 'Oh, I would love it. Where is it?'

'In town, in Church Street, Kensington,' Mr de Gruyt answered. 'I don't live on the premises, but perhaps you could find a room somewhere. Think about it. I am going to miss my young assistant and Mr Leeds assures me you are very capable.'

Her heart seemed suddenly to sink into her boots. As if her mother would allow that!

'Look, as I said, think about it, and if you decide yes, give me a ring.' He handed her his card.

'Thank you, Mr de Gruyt.' Oh, if only she could, but her mother would never go along with it, especially with the raids and being in the centre of London . . .

She could almost have wept with disappointment, but she smiled up at him.

'Thank you, Mr de Gruyt. I will ring you anyway,' she said.

'Good opportunity for you, Julie,' Mr Leeds said, closing the door behind him. 'I needn't tell you that, but I can understand your parents' worries.' He rubbed his hands together. 'Well, Alice, that went rather well, didn't it?'

That night, in her room, Julie sat down and wrote a long letter to her parents, stressing the importance of working for a prestigious house like de Gruyts – that it was an opportunity that wouldn't come again. She would telephone Mr de Gruyt next day and ask exactly what the job involved.

'Please Mum,' she ended, 'I will be eighteen in August . . .'

Chapter Five

Bob had gone to work, but Nancy hurried out of her little prefab house towards the row of shops hastily put up for the new residents where she knew there was a public telephone. Clutching Julie's letter to her bosom, she was quaking inside, firstly because she was not used to the telephone, and secondly because of what Julie's letter contained.

After her two pennies dropped she heard Mr Leeds' voice.

'John Leeds here.'

She introduced herself. 'Mr Leeds, could I possibly speak to Julie if she is there?'

'Yes, of course you may. I'll get her. Julie, call for you.'

Julie's heart went over. Something had happened . . .

Nancy waded straight in. 'Julie, it's me – Mum – I got your letter. Whatever are you thinking of?'

'About the job, you mean? Well, it's such an opportunity – you can ask Mr Leeds—'

'I daresay it is, but you can't stay down there on your own. Now Julie, be sensible. They say when the raids come it will be terrible.'

Julie sighed. 'But we don't know that, do we?'

'Besides, have you thought where you would live? You can't afford to live there on your own with or without a war on. Oh, I do wish you'd be sensible, Julie, you are such a worry.'

'Eileen lives in London on her own.'

'Eileen is a lot older than you, and she earns good money.'

'Well, I could at least go up and see what the job entails, if there would be wages ...'

'Wages! I should hope so! Now, Julie, be a good girl and put the idea to one side. Your dad and I are looking forward to your coming home. You'll like it up here, Julie, honestly.'

'I've got to go – bye, Mum.'

She put the telephone down, her lip trembling.

Mr Leeds smiled at her sympathetically. 'Your mother doesn't approve of the idea of your working for Mr de Gruyt.'

'No.'

'Well, I can understand that. I should probably feel the same if you were my daughter – although there would be no harm in your going up there to see him and asking him more about it. Why don't you go tomorrow? I can manage here.'

Her blue eyes were shining. 'Could I?'

'Yes, telephone him. I'll give you the number.'

So the scene was set.

The appointment at Mr de Gruyt's premises in Church Street was made for ten-thirty and Julie walked to the station in great excitement. Having arrived at Charing Cross, she made her way down to the tube and caught a train to Notting Hill Gate. So far Mr Leeds' instructions were perfect.

She walked down Church Street until she came to the

59

prestigious House of de Gruyt, which was announced in gold lettering above the shop. Peering through the special anti-blast grilles she could see the salon went back a long way, and it was filled with exquisite pieces of furniture, wonderful clocks, and Oriental items. Her heart beating wildly, she pushed open the door.

It was like Aladdin's cave inside.

Seated at a magnificent polished desk was a middle-aged man who looked up when she entered and, getting to his feet, came towards her, smiling.

'Can I help you?' He was tall and slim, and wore a pale fawn-coloured suit and looked so different from most men Julie knew.

'I am Miss Halliwell. I have an appointment with Mr de Gruyt at ten-thirty.'

He smiled at her. 'I am Cecil Carruthers, assistant to Mr de Gruyt. How do you do?' He held out his hand. 'Would you come this way?'

She followed him down to the end of the long gallery, where he turned off into an office.

He tapped on the glass door. 'Maurice, it's Miss Halliwell.'

Maurice de Gruyt rose to his feet.

'Ah, Julie, come in, and sit down,' he indicated a chair. 'You had no difficulty finding us?'

'No, Mr Leeds gave me the directions.'

He saw opposite him a tall, fair-haired girl, neatly dressed and slim; she had quite an air about her, as he had noticed when he first saw her. She looked relaxed, although he was sure she wasn't.

'Now let me tell you about the position here. The young man who has recently left had been with me for three years; he has enlisted in the RAF. His work consisted of running the office, bills, payments, bills of lading, post, that sort of thing, and, of course, he had a degree in fine arts – I expect you don't have that,' he smiled at her.

'No, I'm afraid I have no qualifications. It was my first experience after school in Mr Leeds' shop. But I am very interested and prepared to learn.'

'There is a great deal to learn in this trade,' he said. 'It takes a lifetime. My father started this business and left it to me when he died. I have two assistants who buy in for me and attend sales, older men who I hope will not be called up yet. They have been with the firm for years – but I need someone to take Digby's place in the office, general dogsbody, I suppose you would say.' He smiled apologetically.

'The main problem is that my parents have been moved to Yorkshire owing to the war, and expect me to join them up there; but I must admit, I would like to stay here, in London.'

'Where would you live?' he asked. 'I understand you had been staying at Mr Leeds' house.'

'Oh, it was just a temporary measure,' Julie explained.

'Perhaps you could find a room somewhere? Although there is plenty of space here it is filled with furniture and we couldn't have you living on your own in the present climate. Are you worried about air raids?'

Her blue eyes met his. 'No, but then I've rarely experienced one, just the odd raid now and again.'

'If you came to work for me your wages would be three pounds a week. It's not a lot to live on and it would depend on where you lived. Have you no relatives in London at all?'

'My sister lives in Notting Hill,' Julie said, the idea just coming to her and being discarded almost at once.

'That would be very convenient; could she put you up?'

'I shouldn't think so,' she answered, with a lopsided smile.

'I see ... Well,' he stood up. 'That's the outline, I think enough to let you see what's involved. As you can see, I have a lot of stock, but this is not all of it. It will give you something to work at won't it, and will give you a chance to learn the business. Will you let me know within a few days, because otherwise I shall have to start advertising?'

'Of course,' Julie nodded, standing up to take the hand he offered her. He had a warm handclasp which was re-assuring, 'Thank you, Mr de Gruyt, I will let you know,' and walked out on air.

He watched her go to the door escorted by Cecil Carruthers. He couldn't help wishing there was some way she could take the job. She was intelligent, and very keen, and she looked right. She held herself well, and had wonderful hair. Then he told himself he was getting over-excited at the thought of a pretty young woman working for de Gruyt's after the staid and sober Digby.

Well, it was in the lap of the gods.

Julie found herself outside, not sure what to do next. She walked down Church Street looking in the windows and thinking hard. Suppose – just suppose she telephoned Eileen? What harm would it do? She could say either yes or no, and while she had no wish to live with her sister, nevertheless it might do as a stop-gap. Seeing a red tele-phone box on the other side of the road, she crossed over, and once inside dialled Eileen's office number.

It seemed to take ages to get through to her, but she did finally answer in her usual abrupt way. 'Who?' Julie could hear the irritation in her voice. 'Julie?'

'Your sister,' Julie said patiently. She had never tele-phoned Eileen before, then could hear the consternation in her sister's voice. 'It's all right – there's nothing wrong, it's just that I am in Kensington, and I wondered if I might see you.'

Julie could imagine the frown. 'In Kensington? What are you doing there?'

'I'll tell you when I see you. Can we meet?'

'Well, I'm due for lunch at twelve-thirty. I'll meet you outside Derry and Toms. Can you hang about until then?'

'Of course I can.' Julie's voice betrayed none of the excitement she felt.

She explored the shops until lunch-time, and then there was Eileen coming towards her. She stood out because of her ordinariness, Julie thought. Plain tweed suit, felt hat jammed on her head, no make-up, flat sensible shoes ...

They kissed briefly, a peck more like.

'Well, this is a surprise,' Eileen said. 'We'll go inside to the restaurant. I only have a snack at lunchtime.'

'That'll do me,' Julie said. She was enjoying herself no end.

'So what are you doing here?' Eileen asked when they had ordered.

'I've been after a job,' Julie said.

'Here?' Eileen frowned. 'You must be mad. Does Mum know?'

'Yes.'

'You'd better tell me all about it,' Eileen said looking very severe. You'd never think she was only twenty-two, Julie thought – more like forty.

And she told her; at the end Eileen sat at first open-mouthed then snapped her lips closed in a thin line.

'You're out of your mind!' she said at last. 'At your age, with a war on, and bombs falling. Just where would you live – just tell me that?' and she attacked her Welsh rarebit with gusto.

'I wondered,' Julie began tentatively, 'whether I could stay with you – just for the time being?'

Eileen stared at her. 'Are you serious? I have a one-room basement flat.'

Julie decided to appeal to Eileen's better nature – if she had one.

'Look Eileen – this is such an opportunity for me. I know I could do it, and it's what I want to do. I'm not clever like you and this job would suit me down to the ground. And I don't want to go up to Yorkshire. Can you imagine what it will be like up there, with just Mum and Dad? I'd have to get a job.'

''Course you would – or be called up,' Eileen said.

She seemed to weaken slightly. 'I suppose I could do it for a few days, but then you'd have to get a room of your own, and although there are plenty about at the moment could you afford it on three pounds a week? You'd have to pay twenty-five shillings for a room; then there's the lighting and heating and your food ... It's not on, Julie.'

'Oh, please, Eileen, just for a little while, just so that I don't have to go up to Yorkshire. The Leeds are going off to Cornwall soon and Mr de Gruyt needs an answer.'

'What's he like, this Mr de Gruyt?' Eileen asked suspiciously.

'Oh, such a nice man! It's his own business; it belonged to his father.'

'Yes, you said ...' She collected her handbag and gloves. 'I have to go. I'll pay the bill. Look, since you are up here come round to the flat this evening – I shall be there at six and you might as well see it. Retrace your steps back up Church Street to Notting Hill Gate, and this is the address. Wait outside for me at six.'

Julie heaved a great sigh of relief watching her sister's retreating back. So far so good; she'd never imagined getting this far. And as she wandered in and out of the big stores in the High Street, she thought yes, this was where she wanted to be ...

She saw Eileen coming along the dingy street as she waited outside number forty-one. It couldn't have been a more unprepossessing area, but Julie wasn't about to mind that. Eileen swung her keys and led her down the basement steps, and into a very dark hall and room beyond. A window looked up to the people walking on the pavement outside, and the room wasn't a bad size – it held a divan bed and two easy chairs, a sofa and a sideboard. A small table and two chairs stood beneath the window. Eileen hung her hat and coat behind the door. 'Well, sit down, make yourself at home.' Julie wondered what her mother would think of Eileen's so-called London flat. It was dingier even than Balmoral Street.

'There's a little bathroom and toilet down there. You might want to wash your hands – and the kitchenette is through there. As you will see I haven't much room.'

That was true, Julie thought. How could she stay here? Sleep on the sofa? It really wasn't fair to expect Eileen to help her.

She made her way to the minute bathroom and washed, feeling fresher now than she had all day. She put her head inside the kitchen, which had no window, but was small and neatly kept – trust Eileen.

'We'll go along the road and have something to eat; I haven't anything in the flat.'

'Oh, that's all right,' Julie said. 'I'm not hungry.'

'Well, you should be,' retorted Eileen, 'you didn't have much lunch.'

She sat down opposite Julie and lit a cigarette, which

65

was the first surprise, and exhaled a long stream of smoke. This seemed to relax her, and she took a deep breath.

'I've been thinking. It's only an idea, mind, but if you're so set on this thing, perhaps you could stay here for a few days, but no more than a fortnight. Then we can look around for a room for you somewhere near. I do understand how you feel, oddly enough. I couldn't think of leaving London myself, except of course when the raids come we shall be evacuated down to Hampshire. If you manage to find a basement room, you're as safe there as you would be anywhere and there are plenty of public shelters – not that I'd ever use one . . .'

'Oh, Eileen, could I? Really?'

'Well, it's worth a try. Now the only place you could sleep is on that chair which happens to be a bedchair. You would have to fold it up before you left and let it down again. Well, as I say, it's an emergency and only for a few days. What do you say?'

Julie wanted to hug her sister but refrained from doing so.

'Golly, thanks, Eileen, you're a brick. I'll try not to be a nuisance.'

'First sign of any trouble and you're out,' Eileen said. 'Well that's settled. Let's go and get something to eat and I'll see you to the station. What sort of reception you'll get from Mum and Dad I can't think, but that's your problem, not mine – if you will stick your neck out.'

Julie didn't mind how much Eileen rabbited on now that she had her own way. She would telephone Mr de Gruyt tomorrow and tell him she would take the job and would start on Monday.

'All right if I move in on Monday then?' she asked.

66

'Yes, and for God's sake don't bring much stuff – you can see how I'm placed.'

'I won't,' Julie promised.

On the train going home, Julie made up her mind. She would go up to Yorkshire on Friday and stay overnight. That would give her time to get packed and ready for her exciting new life. It was only fair, she couldn't tell her parents on the phone.

That week she put everything in motion and gave in her notice to Mr Leeds, who was pleased that she had taken the job. They were due to leave London in three weeks and pleased that she had decided to go and see her parents. She sent a telegram to tell them to expect her and was told to take a coach from York station to the village of Denby where they lived.

It was the furthest Julie had ever been away from London and the journey seemed to go on for hours. The countryside rolled away, hills and downs, sheep grazing and everywhere cows. Here and there a station, and she was pleased at last to find herself on the coach at York which serviced the small towns and villages.

At first she couldn't believe it when the conductor called out Denby. It was miles from anywhere: a bus stop, a row of newly built shops and a small new development of prefabricated houses which she guessed was where her parents lived.

Thank heavens she hadn't decided to join them! She would go mad up here ... but there was her dad waiting at the bus stop; she threw her arms around him, almost in tears at the sight of him.

'There's my girl!' he said and, taking her arm and her small suitcase, he led her along new pathways until they came to number fifty-six. There Nancy stood in the doorway, looking so thrilled Julie could scarcely believe it. She enveloped Julie in a bear-like hug, the first Julie could remember for a long time, causing her to feel more guilty than ever.

Nancy led them in proudly. Certainly it was spotlessly clean and new and there was a tiny garden, and seeing that they had all come from the same place they knew most of their neighbours.

'It's lovely,' lied Julie. From the kitchen came the smell of a roast and the table had been laid for three. On a dresser sat a cake, made in her honour, she knew. After being shown around and into the tiny boxroom where she would sleep, they sat down to the meal.

'It was a lovely surprise, your telegram, it gave me a fright at first until I saw the message.' She put the roast potatoes and peas on the table.

'I wanted to give you some notice.'

'But why have you to go back tomorrow? I thought you'd be staying.'

'After supper I'll tell you all about it,' Julie said.

'I hope you haven't done something silly,' Nancy said, taking the succulent joint out of the oven. 'Ready, Bob!' she called.

After they had eaten and cleared away they sat in silence as Julie unfolded her story, Nancy growing paler by the minute.

'I simply can't believe that you have done all this behind our backs,' she said bitterly.

'Not really, Mum, I did tell you about it.'

'And I told you how ridiculous the idea was. Now you say you've seen Eileen and she's going to help you. I am surprised at Eileen, encouraging you, I must say.'

Julie decided that the least said, soonest mended.

'What's it like – Eileen's flat?' Curiosity got the better of Nancy.

'Very nice; small, but comfortable.'

'And this man you're going to work for – how old is he? A young man, elderly? Is he married?'

Julie sighed. 'I don't know, Mum, I didn't ask. I mean, that's his business, but he is a friend of Mr Leeds.'

'The important thing is about the air raids,' Bob said. 'Down there on your own—'

'But I'll be with Eileen.'

'There is that, Bob,' Nancy said. 'I'd be pleased if they were together.'

'I thought Eileen said she'd be evacuated to Hampshire if the raids were heavy?'

'Oh, I don't know,' Nancy said. Julie decided to bring the argument to a close.

'Well, I've done it now, I've accepted the position, I start on Monday and go straight to Eileen's after work.'

Nancy opened her mouth to say something but Bob shook his head at her. 'Seems it's all settled, then,' and he got up and walked out.

'You've really upset your dad this time,' Nancy said.

'I know, I'm sorry, Mum,' and she was.

Then, typically, Nancy set to work organising what Julie would take with her and what she would leave at home.

'Everything of yours is up here, except what you took to Mr Leeds.'

'Eileen says I mustn't take much for she hasn't the room.'

'Well you won't need heavy clothes, and I would like you to have bought a new dress to start work with. You haven't had one since you left school. I'll give you some money to take back.'

Impulsively, Julie, having got her own way all along the line, rushed over to her mother and kissed her.

'Thanks, Mum,' she said.

'Oh, get off with you,' Nancy said. 'I expect Eileen will help you choose something nice.'

Not if I can help it, thought Julie.

Chapter Six

Julie arrived on Eileen's doorstep at eight-thirty on a Monday morning in June.

'Eileen, could I leave my suitcase? I'll unpack it tonight.'

'Lucky you caught me, I was just leaving. Put it in the hall for now.'

'Thanks, Eileen, see you later.'

'Bye, and good luck.'

That was nice of her, thought Julie, and hurried on down to Church Street. She rang the bell and it was answered by a motherly woman who let her in.

'Good morning, I'm Miss Halliwell.'

'Hello, dear, and I'm Mrs Mackenzie. Mr de Gruyt told me to expect you. I come in from eight until nine-thirty or so every day so anything you want just ask me. Hang your coat in this cupboard and I'll show you where the cloakroom is. Mr de Gruyt doesn't usually arrive until nine-thirty so you can wait in the office. You know your way?'

'Yes, thank you,' and hanging up her coat and checking herself in the mirror, Julie made her way there.

Somehow she wasn't half as nervous as she had been when she started at Mr Leeds' shop, but the sound of the air-raid siren startled her.

'If we heard anything we'd go down into the basement,' Mrs Mackenzie said, 'but I expect it's another false alarm. They get through you know, the odd raider. Let's hope it doesn't get any worse, eh?' and humming to herself, she flicked her feather duster over the furniture.

Julie glanced round the office, and it was then that Maurice de Gruyt came in and greeted her.

'Good morning, Miss Julie. I hope you have made yourself at home? I'll be with you in a moment.'

He hurried away and returned in a few minutes. 'Are we in the middle of an alert?' he asked, and when Julie smiled and nodded, asked her to take the seat opposite him.

'Now, first of all, I would like you to familiarize yourself with the premises. We are on four floors here, three and the basement, and I have cleared the basement somewhat in order that we may go down there in the event of raids. It is burglar-proof, supposedly sound-proof and reinforced with concrete. We have chairs to sit on and mattresses in case of night raids, and emergency rations – so let's just hope they won't be necessary, eh?'

At this point the 'All clear' sounded, but neither took any notice.

'Now, I'd like you to walk around the showrooms and explore. You will quickly assess the kind of stuff we specialize in, get the feel of the place, examine and above all ask questions. It is the only way to learn! Over there you will find reference books on almost every subject – please feel free to browse through them. There will be some office work, of course, letters and post to deal with. A lot of our correspondence is from abroad – or at least it was before the war. I shall expect you to welcome buyers, especially the dealers, who you will get to know in time; some of them call in every week, some once a month – the Americans perhaps every three months or so. You've met my assistant Mr Carruthers, the other one is travelling in Scotland at the moment. Now have you any questions?'

'I just hope I give satisfaction,' Julie said. 'I feel very inexperienced.'

'Oh, you'll learn quickly – the antiques world appeals to you, does it?'

'I didn't know much about it before I went to work for Mr Leeds, but I love beautiful things, and colour. I find I get quite excited by colour.'

'Then you are in the right place,' he smiled. 'Now off you go, start on the top floor, it's mainly furniture up there, and work your way down.'

He watched her go. Yes, she was young, barely eighteen. What had his mother said? 'Baby-snatching, Maurice?' and recognized it for what it was, an apprehension that he might fall for this young English girl after always employing male staff. Well, it would be easy enough, but he wasn't a fool. The difference in their ages was all too apparent and at twenty-eight he was not about to make a fool of himself even though he knew his mother wanted him to marry and settle down. To carry on the name of de Gruyt, in the main. It was understandable.

Julie made her way up carpeted stairs to the top floor, seeing the great chandeliers lit even at this time of day casting a glow over the furniture. If Mrs Mackenzie kept all this polished she certainly did a good job. She looked at the price tags, discreetly hidden, and gasped at some of the prices, and wondered not for the first time what she was doing here in this prestigious gallery having come from somewhere like Balmoral Street.

She took her time and made her way down to the second floor just as the air-raid siren went again. On this floor stood huge Chinese urns and great vases, fine English china in polished dressers and on shelves, and wonderful paintings lined the walls ... How awful if the raids started in earnest. She walked down to the ground floor, her slim hand on the polished banister rail, and saw that Mr de Gruyt was with a client. They were examining a grandfather clock; she made her way to the office and busied herself with the reference books, becoming quickly absorbed.

The alert was still on when he came back to the office, and asked her to sort through the post. Afterwards he dictated some letters, each one with three copies, which kept her busy until lunch-time when the 'All clear' sounded again.

Somehow the time went quickly; he had told her the hours would be nine-thirty until five. She found plenty to do each day just with the office work, filing and typing letters, looking through catalogues for items she had been asked to mark off. Sometimes she greeted a customer if Mr de Gruyt was not available and asked them to wait, all the time learning and absorbing knowledge about this new and attractive business.

On Saturday she bought herself a new dress, and on Sunday went over to see Gwen, meeting in the church and going for a walk in the park.

'No Les or Martin today,' Gwen said. There was no one on the tennis courts.

'How is your mother getting on in Devon?' Julie asked.

'Oh, she's all right, I'm a bit bored with you gone,' Gwen said. 'What do you do with yourself? What's he like, this Mr—?'

74

'de Gruyt? Oh, he's a very nice man.'

'Elderly, isn't he?'

'Well, I shouldn't think he's thirty yet.'

'That's what I said – elderly.' They got up from the seat and walked on.

'My dad says the raids are hotting up, and he doesn't give much away as you know.'

'Really?'

'Yes, he says the dog-fights over the coast are tremendous and we've lost ever such a lot of planes. The Germans have got us ringed round from Norway to France with only the Channel in between. We can hear it all from where we are in south London.'

She glanced at Julie curiously. 'I mean if they do get here—'

'They won't,' Julie said.

'But if they do, you can't stay there in the thick of it all.'

'Neither can you,' Julie retorted.

'I'd go down to Devon, I suppose.'

'Poor you. Well, I'd better be off if I'm to catch my train.'

'It was lovely to see you,' Gwen said. 'By the way, we're on the telephone now – wait – I'll give you my number. We'll be able to keep in touch.'

'Oh, that's lovely,' Julie said, and going home in the train realized how much she missed Gwen.

Julie found Eileen sitting on the floor in the living room obviously having a turn-out.

'You're back,' she said. 'How was Gwen?'

'All right; what are you doing?'

'What does it look as if I'm doing? I know you won't be staying long, but I thought I'd shift some things around to make more room.'

'Oh, you didn't have to.'

'Well, as you know, I'm a bit pushed for space, and I need room for storage, so if you like to put what clothes you've got alongside mine in this side of the wardrobe, then I can have the other side for storage.' Julie saw the key in the lock.

'Yes, OK. I haven't brought much with me.'

'Good thing, too. By the way, I won't be going down to Hampshire if the worst comes to the worst. I've been seconded – I can't tell you where, but it's important.'

'In London?' Julie asked.

'Yes, in London,' Eileen said, and Julie knew that was the end of the matter.

'It might be a good idea if you looked around for a bedsit,' she said. 'There're plenty about and you'll be better on your own. You need a room in a basement – it's safer.'

'Yes,' said Julie. 'I'll start looking.'

She made a few sporadic attempts during the lunch hour and had to admit she was half-hearted about it. Eileen wasn't such a bad old sport when you got to know her, her bark was worse than her bite. Still, she seemed adamant about Julie finding somewhere of her own to live and truth to tell it would be better for her. She posted a letter to her mother and on her way to Church Street thought about Maurice de Gruyt. He was such an attractive man. If she were older it would be quite easy to fall for him. She still had a sneaking regard for Les Daly, but now when she thought of him he seemed so young. Still, perhaps in any case Maurice de Gruyt was married. He had no photographs in his office and there was no way of knowing if he was.

Towards the end of June he went away for a week, and told her he was going to the West Country and attending auctions. The other assistant, a younger man called Mark Clayton came back to see her.

'A young lady!' he said on being introduced. 'Now that is a turn-up for the book! Just ask me anything you want to know, Julie, is it?'

Julie was glad to see a friendly face. Mr Carruthers tended to be very serious-minded. But she got on with her job, examining everything, and reading up about it, and sometimes wondering how the gallery coped in these hard times. Trade was very poor – Mr Leeds' little shop had been bustling by comparison. She realized Mr de Gruyt needed a junior to keep the office going. Nevertheless, how long would it continue if the rumours flying about were true that invasion was imminent?

As July approached the rumours and the air-raid warnings became stronger. It was said that the Germans intended to invade and had decided to begin their offensive in July. The air battles over the Channel were extensive, leading to the loss of many planes on both sides, and the Luftwaffe bombed every ship in sight. It was growing nearer day by day – the Battle of Britain had started.

Maurice de Gruyt decided at this juncture that they should use the basement more often. He had a responsibility to staff and now, when the sirens sounded, he locked the front door and they went down to the basement. They could hear distant gunfire and planes overhead despite the sound-proofing, and although he tried to hide his concern, nevertheless he was worried for Julie.

'Make some coffee, will you, Julie?' he said one day. 'You must call me Maurice. This is not the time for standing on ceremony. And you must tell me if you are in the least bit worried. I shall quite understand, if you feel ...'

But Julie, to be honest, found it rather exciting.

She loved these sessions, which became quite regular, when she and Maurice went down to the basement, sometimes three times a day depending on how many alerts there were. Sometimes Mr Carruthers or Mark Clayton joined them, but business seemed to be at a standstill. Then Mark announced that he was going to enlist. 'If they'll have me,' he grinned.

'I shall be sorry to lose you,' Maurice said.

That long morning he and Julie talked. He told her of his background, that he had lived in London with his parents, and now with his widowed mother in Inverness Square in London and they had a housekeeper who took good care of her. Of how his father had come over from Holland; he was an art expert, and married an English girl, and he, their only child, had been born in 1912. So he is twenty-eight, Julie thought, not that old ...

Julie talked about her life at home in Balmoral Street, such an area being a total mystery to someone of Maurice's background. But he loved to watch the way her eyes sparkled when she talked about her father, or her friends; she was very descriptive and they passed many pleasant interludes.

As August approached he knew he had to make a decision. Bombs had already been dropped on Bristol and on aerodromes in Kent, the Luftwaffe were intent on destroying the Royal Air Force, and now they were making for London itself.

It wasn't fair to keep her working up here in such danger. He knew he had grown fond of her – and it wasn't as if the business was doing well.

*

One evening in early August Julie arrived home early and began to prepare an evening meal. Going to the wardrobe to find her wedge shoes after being on high heels all day, she noticed the key in the lock on Eileen's storage side of the wardrobe again, and curiosity got the better of her. What does she keep in there, she wondered? It was always kept locked, but now she turned the key, and stepped back with a gasp.

Inside was a complete airman's uniform – that of an officer – fur-lined boots, shaving tackle, soap and tooth-brush, well-pressed trousers on the hanging rail, another jacket with a pair of wings up, shirts – Air Force blue – shoes, slippers . . . She closed the door swiftly, her face flaming, and locked it, subsiding on to a chair in dis-belief.

Eileen – Eileen – she had always been secretive, but she knew she couldn't face her sister at this stage. Hurriedly, she put the food away in the larder and left a note: 'Gone to look at a flat. Love Julie.' She just couldn't face her sister.

Julie walked around for what seemed like hours until the raid became quite heavy and she went into the station where people were already tucked down for the night, stepping over recumbent bodies until the 'All clear' sounded, knowing the siren would go off again later when it got quite dark. She was still in a state of shock, having accepted the fact that her sister Eileen was not quite all she appeared to be. Her mother and father mustn't know – they would be horrified . . . And how was she to face her? No wonder her own arrival had been such a shock. It had been jolly nice of her to accept the situation, considering. And where was the Air Force officer based? Of course she wanted Julie to find a place of her own; it was only natural.

Eileen was at home when she finally got back, and looked up, eyeing her. 'How did you get on? I was worried about you.'

'I went down into the station.'

'Ugh,' Eileen said. 'What about the flat?'

'No, nothing doing, but I have hopes of one to-morrow,' she said, adding, 'I'll go in my lunch-hour,' knowing full well she was lying. But from then on she was determined to find something, however basic.

Then the night raids started. The warning would go in the early evening and sometimes last all night until the 'All clear' sounded in the early hours. Then it was a case of dragging yourself up after a noisy and probably sleepless night.

Maurice had to do some deep thinking. Loath as he was to close the business at this stage of events there was not much point in opening the gallery. Business was hardly moving, the London raids coinciding with the raids over Germany. Battles were taking place overhead and he knew he had a duty to his staff on the one hand to keep going, on the other a regard for their physical safety.

His mother was concerned for him. 'What are you going to do, Maurice?' she asked gently. 'No one wants to give in to these monsters, but don't you think you should close the gallery for the time being? This bombing cannot go on for ever, and how is that little girl taking it?'

She asked this because she knew he thought about the girl a great deal more than he let on. She was curious about her; after all, it was not all that unusual for a man of Maurice's age to fall for a young girl. She herself had married an older man at nineteen – and a Dutchman at that, much to her family's disapproval. If it hadn't been that he was such a gentleman and a famous art expert her family might not have given their consent. She had never regretted it, only the lack of a girl in her son's life.

There had been a girl once, in his early twenties, who was quite obviously mad about him; she would have been a suitable bride, but nothing had come of it. Well, she mustn't run away with herself. This girl had a most unsuitable background, from what she had gathered.

That evening while they sat in the basement, she could feel the tenseness in him and knew it was not about the raids so much as worrying about Julie.

'Why don't you invite her to dinner one evening?'

He turned shocked eyes to her. 'To dinner?'

'Yes, we could do with some company and she might just as well stay in our basement as her own. What do you think?' and saw his eyes light up with sheer pleasure at the prospect.

'Yes, that sounds a wonderful idea – cheer things up a bit. When do you suggest?'

'Tomorrow, Friday – either suits me.'

'When the 'All clear' sounded at seven twenty-five in the morning he raced up the basement steps two at a time.

When Julie told Eileen that she had been invited to dinner by Mrs de Gruyt, Eileen looked suspicious.

'His mother?' she repeated. 'What's the idea? And what will you do when the siren goes?'

'They have a basement, I suppose we will go down there.'

'Well, get home if you can. If he is a gentleman he should bring you home,' and she sniffed her disapproval. 'You know, Julie, I don't want to be difficult, but this isn't easy for me. I'm used to being on my own and it's a bit cramped with the two of us.' She didn't meet Julie's eyes.

'I know, it's really been very good of you.' Julie didn't know where to look.

'Perhaps I could give you a hand looking? I'll ask around the office.'

'Well, there was one bedsit in Notting Hill – I think I'll go back there and have another look.' Julie lied. She would take almost anything, and truth to tell she hadn't looked far up to now.

Eileen brightened considerably.

On Friday evening Julie looked her best. Her face slightly flushed at the prospect of the evening in front of her, she was in her element as Maurice took her arm while getting into the taxi which drove them to Inverness Square.

She had never been inside such a London house before, and although it contained priceless paintings as even she could see, it had none of the richness and furniture of the Leeds' house. Mrs de Gruyt turned out to be a tall, slim woman with white hair, and a fine bearing, who greeted Julie in a friendly manner.

'Well, Julie I've been looking forward to meeting you,' she said taking both her hands. As a matter of fact Julie was quite different from what she had expected. A south London girl from a poor area, Mrs de Gruyt was pleasantly surprised.

'How do you do?' Julie said observing at once that Maurice did not get his vivid blue eyes from his mother, who had rather sad dark eyes.

'I thought we would eat at once,' his mother said. 'Before the air-raid siren goes. What do you think, Maurice?'

'Good idea,' he said taking Julie's coat and gloves. 'We'll dispense with a pre-dinner drink, have some wine with the meal? All right, Julie?'

She nodded happily, pleased to be where she was after being cooped up in Eileen's flat, and the less she thought about that situation the better. She still hadn't got over the shock of her discovery.

The housekeeper served dinner in the dining room, a room bolted and barred with iron grilles.

'I hope you like lamb,' Mrs de Gruyt said. 'It is Mrs Jones' speciality.'

Julie smiled. Not for nothing was she an aspiring actress, listening to the radio non-stop in order to perfect her vowel sounds and to learn how to pronounce words properly. She had watched the Leeds family at table and she was keen to learn. After all, if she was going to be an actress ... She thought, not for the first time, how far away that dream seemed now, and not so important. There were other things in life.

She watched Maurice's elegant hands as he poured the wine, seeing the fine golden hairs; and looking up, she caught his eye, surprised to find herself somewhat disconcerted. She knew she liked him, admired him, but was unprepared for the sudden feeling of warmth which flooded through her at his close proximity.

They had got as far as the dessert when the air-raid siren went and without further ado, Mrs de Gruyt got to her feet. 'We'll have coffee downstairs,' she said. 'This way, Julie.'

They had hardly reached the basement when there was the most horrific explosion, and it sounded very near. All the lights went out at once, and Maurice miraculously produced a torch to show them their way. Once in the basement, they lit candles and, joined by Mrs Jones, settled down for what would appear to be a long night.

So far it was the worst night raid of the war; they could hear the bombs dropping, and what might have been planes being shot out of the sky. The house itself shook, windows rattled, the 'crump crump' of the bombs falling one after another. It didn't do to imagine what kind of mess they would find in the morning if they survived the night . . .

In the early hours, Mrs de Gruyt and Mrs Jones slept on mattresses covered with blankets, leaving Maurice and Julie together and it seemed the most natural thing for him to take Julie's hand in his.

Presently he lit fresh candles and they dozed, waking to the sound of the 'All clear' at seven in the morning.

Mrs Jones was already up and had made tea and coffee with powdered milk. Maurice released Julie's hand, still in his. 'Stay there,' he said, 'I'm going upstairs.'

She missed the warmth of his hand, it had been so comforting, but now, she too got up: 'I'm coming with you.'

The house was full of dust, a thick haze over everything, but Maurice went straight to the door and opened it, to be met outside with a sea of rubble and glass, and what looked like a pea-soup fog. There were ambulance men and fire engines and Home Guards in the Square while an acrid smell hung over everything. Behind him, Julie took his arm.

'Eileen,' she gasped, 'Maurice, I must go—'

He slammed the door behind him. 'I'm coming with you.'

Hand in hand they trod over the piles of concrete and rubble, the dust filling their lungs.

It seemed to take hours to go the short distance to Eileen's flat, so difficult was it to walk among the debris,

84

but turning the corner there was no doubt about what had happened. Eileen's building was no longer there.

Turning, with a stifled cry, Julie threw herself into Maurice's arms, and he held her tightly, closely, until she stopped shaking.

When she finally raised her head, her blue eyes were blank, her face as white as a sheet, her lips bloodless.

'There's nothing we can do here – you're coming home with me, and I shall make all the inquiries – you won't have to do a thing.'

She couldn't find a word to say, just followed him as, holding her hand tightly, he led the difficult way back to Church Street, which seemed to have got off lightly this time, and thence to Inverness Square.

Once inside, he poured her a glass of brandy. 'Come on, it won't hurt you, you've had a shock.'

She drank it down, and it burned her throat. She set the glass on the table.

'I must go home,' she said. 'I must go home to my parents, Maurice. At once – they will be devastated. I'm sorry, they thought the world of Eileen – oh, how terrible for them—' and she burst into tears.

'Not just yet,' he said. 'I'll take you to the station, but it might not be easy, I don't know if the trains are running.'

'I'll take a chance,' she said. 'I have to go— I'll get home somehow. I'm sorry – please don't come with me – I can find my way. I'm sorry, Maurice—'

'Wait—'

But she was hurrying away. He watched her disappear through the haze of dust and smoke, then turned back towards Notting Hill where Eileen had lived . . .

Chapter Seven

Julie had been home in Yorkshire a week – a dreadful week when she had grown closer to her parents than she had ever been before – and knew she would not leave them now. It was a nightmare.

When Nancy Halliwell saw Julie standing on the doorstep looking dishevelled and without any luggage she knew there was something terribly wrong. Once inside and Julie had sobbed out her pitiful story Nancy sat still and white-faced, unable to believe what she had heard. There were so many questions she wanted to ask, such as why was Julie away from home, realizing with horror that Julie also might have been killed by that terrible blast if she had been in the flat. Bob took the news very badly, his grief compounded by guilt that Julie had always been his favourite daughter. Only a telegram from Maurice de Gruyt confirmed what he and Julie had already known. The bombs had devastated the block of flats, and of Eileen there was no trace. The official information came much later.

Julie, with just her handbag to show for her brief London stay, wrote to Maurice, thanking him for all his help. She wished him and his mother well, and told him that she would be staying in Yorkshire with her parents, probably for the duration of the war.

The three of them clung together trying to come to terms with their loss, with the knowledge that they were out of their usual environment. But it wasn't a bad place, Julie realised, there was a lot to be said for the small community of exiles, thrown together through no wish of their own. The countryside was picturesque and although Bob's factory was a long way off, nevertheless, their home was not too far from York, which Julie thought a beautiful city.

She realized that she would soon have to get a job; even Nancy spent a few hours a week at the Forces canteen. They went out to the local pub for a drink on her eighteenth birthday, something they would never have done at home.

Julie thought longingly of Maurice de Gruyt and his beautiful premises in London. Of his home in Inverness Square, and how removed from it all she was up here. Still, she didn't intend to live like this always and the war would not last for ever.

With Julie's departure, Maurice found it increasingly difficult to settle. The whole business seemed to have taken on a new aspect; not only was the gallery doing virtually no business, but the whole idea of antiques and luxury goods seemed out of place in wartime.

The moment had come, he felt, when he wanted to do something more useful, make some kind of contribution to the war effort. His contacts were many and, speaking Dutch as he did fluently, Special Intelligence soon found him a niche. It was something that would take him away from home quite often, so plans had to be put into operation. The contents of the gallery were stored, and his mother and her housekeeper moved down to Cornwall, the house in Inverness Square closed.

He wrote to tell Julie of this, and wished her well. Julie thought of his hand covering hers on that dreadful night, and realized that it was an episode in her life that was over. It was time she stood up and faced the facts: she was young and strong and her parents needed her.

As time went by Nancy was able to speak of Eileen, asking questions about Eileen's flat, why Julie herself had not been there on that fateful night.

'You weren't keen on him, were you – that man, what's his name?'

'Maurice?' But Nancy saw how she blushed. Thank God she's home, she thought.

'It's so sad,' she said more than once, referring to Eileen. 'Not yet twenty-three and she never had a chance. Never a chance to marry or have children. I hope she was happy – I know she loved her work.'

Julie, remembering the RAF uniform, said not a word.

Within two weeks she had found herself a job at the local council offices doing war work. Gwen would have a laugh, she thought, remembering how she had jeered at Gwen with her council job, which reminded her that she owed Gwen a letter. She settled down easily enough; they were a nice bunch and as different from Londoners as chalk and cheese. The job was in the city centre which was very convenient, for she could spend her lunch hours and spare time looking round the city, which never failed to interest her. York Minster and the old wall, the dear little cobbled streets – the pleasures were manifold. Even the shops were different and full of interest. One Saturday afternoon she found a small antique shop tucked away, still open for business although she didn't imagine it did much

trade. She went in, and was reminded of Mr Leeds'
little shop. An elderly man looked over the top of his
glasses at her.

'Just looking?' he asked.

'Yes, although I'd like to see the small plate in the
window – Minton, I think.'

'Certainly,' he said, going to the window and getting it
out.

He looked at her shrewdly. 'A collector, are you?'

She shook her head, and smiled.

'But you recognized a bit of Minton.'

'Before coming up here I had a little training in
antique porcelain.'

'Oh, you did . . .'

She bought the plate, and from then on it became a
weekly visit she looked forward to.

Towards Christmas the old man suggested that she might
like to give him a hand in the shop on Saturday afternoons; he could do with it at this festive time of year.

She was delighted – this was more like it. She took no
money from him, assuring him that it was all part of her
training.

The Christmas card from Gwen that year gave her the
latest news, that she had been to a Christmas party and
guess what? Les Daly was on leave and had seen her
home! He looked absolutely fabulous in his uniform –
like a film star.

Julie put the card on the mantelpiece. She was
surprised that she didn't feel more deeply about Les Daly
and Gwen. But the loss of her sister had overshadowed
everything, especially at Christmas, and she was less
moved than she thought she would be. Balmoral Street
seemed a million miles away.

When the Christmas card came from Maurice, she was delighted. He wrote that he couldn't tell her where he was, but he was doing Special Intelligence work. The address was a cryptic one, but if she would like to write to him and tell him how she was getting on, he would be pleased to hear from her.

With flushed cheeks she took the card up to her room and read it over and over, then she went over to the window which overlooked the ploughed fields and sat in the chair, thinking. Was it possible that she was in love with Maurice de Gruyt, or was she just in love with what he stood for? That he was out of her class was obvious, and the idea of their ever coming together in peacetime was ludicrous.

Yet, he had felt something too. They were friends, if you like. It was nothing like the hot exciting feeling she had felt for Les Daly, but she looked back on that now as something childish. Was it perhaps the fascination of Maurice's business? The fact that his world was the glamorous world of antiques which fascinated her so. It might be better if she tried to forget him and his world. It wasn't as if she needed a father-figure, she had a wonderful father of her own. But at the thought of that elegant man, with the fine gold hairs on the backs of his hands, those eyes which looked at her in a certain way, the way his fair hair fell on his forehead . . .

She sent him a Christmas card and wished him well.

They had a Christmas party at the council offices, sadly bereft of men, because most young men were away at the war. A nice young man wearing glasses took her home, a young man who was passionately keen to do his bit, but was prevented by his bad eyesight. She warmed to him. Also she made friends

90

with a girl called Vanda who was a nurse in the local hospital. She too had come from London and her family lived on the new estate.

It was a bleak January morning when the telegraph boy delivered a telegram addressed to Miss Julie Halliwell.

I SHALL BE PASSING THROUGH YORK ON SUNDAY CAN YOU MEET ME 11.30 YORK STATION. MAURICE.

Julie hugged it to her. Meet him? Of course she could, and would.

'Who is it from?' Nancy asked. She hated telegrams, they almost always brought bad news.

'Maurice de Gruyt; he is coming to York on Sunday and asks if I could meet him.'

'Oh, Julie!'

'What's wrong with that?' Julie asked, belligerent, wanting nothing to stand in her way.

'Why on earth does he want to see you?'

'Mum, he is twenty-eight, and we are friends, that's all.'

'I should hope so,' Nancy said. With just one daughter left she didn't want any problems.

After breakfast Julie took the bus to York Station. With her fur collar pulled up round her neck and matching fur hat she stood out from the crowd, as did Maurice de Gruyt in his khaki officer's uniform.

Her heart leapt when she saw him, and she hurried over to where he stood beneath the clock.

'Julie!' Without standing on ceremony, he kissed her lightly on the cheek.

Her eyes shone as he put his arm through hers. 'It's wonderful to see you, Julie, I had begun to think I would never see you again.' He glanced at his watch. 'I have exactly one hour and a half; could we go somewhere for coffee?'

'Of course.'

'Do we have time to go to an hotel – is there one near by?'

'Yes, across the road.' They hurried towards the entrance of the hotel to the coffee lounge.

'Now, tell me all you have been doing since you arrived up here. Are your parents well? They must have been so glad you came up to join them.'

Julie told him about her job and working at weekends, and he laughed.

'Oh, Julie, it is so good to see you.' He looked into her eyes and she felt herself weakening.

She removed her coat and put it over the back of the sofa.

'How is your mother?' Anything to keep things on an even keel. She had no doubts now about her feelings for him. She felt she had come home and wanted more than anything for him to put his arms around her.

'She is well, but anxious to come back to London. She is no lover of the country.

'And what about you and your job? Is it interesting? Do you have to travel?'

'I'm based in London at the War Office but some-times, like today, I have to make a journey. Julie—'

'Yes?' She daren't meet his eyes.

The waiter brought the coffee.

'Julie,' he took her hand, 'I realize I am older than you—'

She raised wide eyes to his as a swift shaft of excitement mixed with fear ran through her, and to hide her confusion she poured more coffee.

'I am giving you fair notice,' he said seriously. 'I want you to consider marrying me.'

It was the last thing she expected him to say. 'Maurice!'

'I'm sorry – I've shocked you. I haven't even asked you if you have a boyfriend.'

She shook her head. 'No, but it's impossible, Maurice.'

'You mean because I am too old for you?'

'No, not that, but, well, my parents would never agree, and I am sure your mother wouldn't approve. Besides we hardly know each other.'

'I think we do,' he said seriously. 'I've never yet met a girl that I wanted to marry until I met you.'

'I've never given marriage a thought,' said Julie.

'I've rushed you,' he said contritely. 'I never gave a thought to your feelings. I suppose I hoped, well, that we both felt the same . . .'

She looked straight at him, into those vivid blue eyes.

'Could you love me enough to marry me, Julie?'

'Yes, I could,' she said honestly, 'but I think we should give it more time.' She didn't add that if it were not wartime the idea would possibly never have occurred to him.

Sitting next to him like this she knew how strong her feelings were. She was in no doubt that she loved him, but she had never had a proper boyfriend – how did you know when you were in love? She thought briefly about Les Daly: he meant nothing now, yet she had gone hot and cold at the thought of seeing him. This was different.

'I'm really happy to stay friends,' she said.

He shook his head. 'Not enough, Julie, I need a wife – someone to come home to, to share the business with when we get back on our feet after the war.'

'But there are many people qualified to do that,' she said.

'But not as my wife. I would be good to you, Julie, take care of you. Your parents would need to have no fear on that account.'

'You've never even met them,' she smiled, thinking: I wonder what his reaction would be if he came to the little development of prefabricated houses, yet thrilled at the same time that he should ask her to marry him.

At this moment all she wanted was for him to put his arms around her and hold her close. 'It's all too soon,' she said. 'We mustn't rush into this,' and thought how much like Eileen she must be to be so careful. She had always jumped in where angels feared to tread, which was one of the things her mother worried about. Still, she was eighteen now, nineteen this year – old enough to make her own decisions. Strange, she thought, that she felt the older of the two . . .

'I have to think of my parents,' she explained. 'They have only recently lost one precious daughter. I couldn't possibly give them the shock of telling them I am about to leave home to be married. They have never even met you, the shock would be too great, and they would think me too young.'

'I know, I am being selfish and thinking only of myself and what I want, but I feel if you were free you would want it too. Am I right?'

'Yes, but you do understand? Give me time – we'll write to each other, often,' she said, 'get them used to the idea that I have a life too, but I am not going to break it to them before I think the timing is right. By the way, what does your mother think of the idea?'

'I wanted to see what you would say first before—'

'Ahh . . .' she said, and took his hand. 'Quite honestly,

there is nothing I would like more than to run away and marry you.' She saw his eyes light up.

'Julie! Would—'

'No, it's not the best time, but we'll write to each other, and see each other when we can.'

He looked so disappointed that she surprised herself by leaning forward and swiftly kissing him on the cheek.

He caught her hand, and she clasped it in both hers feeling the shock waves like electricity at his touch.

'You will tell your parents about us, won't you?'

'Yes, I will.'

'Promise?'

'I promise,' she said and glanced up at the large clock. 'And now it's time for you to go.'

He glanced at his watch, and helped her on with her coat, tucking her warmly in. He paid the bill and they walked across the road to the station where he took her in his arms and kissed her.

She needed no further evidence as to how she felt. She wanted it to go on for ever, and sighed as she watched him go.

Getting off the bus, she hugged the knowledge to herself that Maurice really loved her, and wanted to marry her. And she would start by telling her mother that they were very close friends and that he wanted to see her again. She could see Nancy quickly put the lace curtain into place as she walked up the path. She would have to play this very carefully. With a bright smile she unlocked the front door and went into the small kitchen, seeing her mother's look of apprehension while she pretended to be getting lunch.

'Did you see him?'

'Maurice? Yes, he was there waiting for me. He only

had an hour and a half, but it was nice to see him again. He looked very grand in his uniform, he's a captain.'

'Your father's in the garden, give him a call.'

Julie took off her coat and hat and went to the back door. 'Dad!'

'So he's a captain,' Nancy said draining the peas.

'Yes.'

'I thought you said he was foreign – how did he get into the British army?' She sounded querulous.

'He was born here, but his father was Dutch. He speaks the language, so I expect he's useful.'

'Ah, Julie, you're back,' Bob said, washing his hands at the sink. 'Did you see the young man?'

'He's not very young, Bob,' Nancy said. 'Julie says he's a captain in the Army,' she added.

Bob made a face. 'Oh. Very nice,' he said. 'Many people about?'

And Julie knew that was that.

Later on that day, however, Nancy could not contain her curiosity. 'Where is he stationed, this . . . Maurice?' She still couldn't get used to the name.

'At the War Office, I think, and he is on some kind of secret service work. I know it's important.'

Nancy bent over her sewing. 'And you say he's not married?'

'No, never has been, and he doesn't have a girlfriend,' except me, she wanted to add.

Nancy re-threaded her needle. 'Funny to get to that age and not be married or engaged.' She lifted guileless eyes to Julie's.

'I don't see why,' Julie said. 'I think the business is very important to him. After all, it is his own, left to him by his father.'

'He'll be well off, then,' Nancy said sensibly.

96

'Who knows what will happen after the war?' Julie said. 'But he is a very nice man – you'd like him, Mum.'

'Would I?' Nancy bit off a thread. She could see nothing but trouble ahead . . .

Chapter Eight

The letters from Maurice came regularly every week. In them he gave Julie as much news as he could of his whereabouts, that he had been down to see his mother in Cornwall, and told her of his wish to marry Julie. She hadn't seemed in the least bit surprised, just asked what Julie's reaction was, and that of her family. He had to point out that her parents as yet were unaware.

'I should persuade Julie to tell them as soon as possible – it is only fair,' his mother said.

He returned to London and wrote another letter to Julie. If only she had been on the telephone things might have been easier.

Sometimes Julie saw Nancy's eyes fill with tears, and knew she was thinking about Eileen. It was then that she wondered whether to reveal to her mother about Eileen's boyfriend. Her mother regretted more than anything that Eileen had had no life other than her job. Would it console her to know that Eileen had had a separate life that none of them knew about? Then again, she knew what her mother's attitude was to immorality, as she saw it. She would be so upset at the idea of her beloved daughter living in sin, as she would call it, that it might blight her memory for ever.

Julie decided to keep a still tongue in a wise head.

The raids continued nationwide – the Baedeker raids, on beautiful cities like Bath, Cheltenham, Bristol, Liverpool and London. Would there never be an end to this terrible bombing? As things got worse during August Julie made up her mind that she would tell them about Maurice, of his desire to marry her. Nancy always eyed the letters, but she never mentioned them. When they came it was as if she thought that ignoring them would make them go away.

One Sunday morning in August, during the height of the London blitz, a stranger made his way to the door of Number Fifty-six Sherwood Gardens, in Denby, near York.

He was dressed in the blue uniform of an RAF officer, and when the door opened, he removed his cap.

Nancy stared at him.

'Mrs Halliwell?' He spoke with an accent, and she could see the word POLISH on his shoulder and a pair of wings on his jacket.

She smiled – he must be lost. 'I don't think you want me. Have you got the right address?'

She looked down at the piece of paper he was carrying, and it flashed through her mind that he might be a German spy pretending to be on their side. All sorts of things happened in this war. You were warned to look out for strangers. Her face grew tense. 'Julie!' she called, and Julie came through from the kitchen.

'Julie, this . . . gentleman is looking for this address. What is your name?'

'Josef,' he said. 'I am Squadron Leader Josef Szarnicki.'

Julie couldn't think why the connection came to her, but it did, in a flash. She had seen a uniform like that before and the colour in her face drained away, while her heart began to beat uncomfortably. Eileen.

'You had better come in,' she said, stony-faced.

'Julie!' Nancy said.

'It's all right, Mum.' He was following Julie into the small front room, a stockily built young man, about thirty, quite good-looking, with hazel eyes and a round face.

She took the bull by the horns. 'Please sit down,' she said, while Nancy stood and stared. 'I think Mr Szarnicki was a friend of Eileen's,' she said. 'Am I right?' And she smiled at him pleasantly.

'Yes,' he smiled, showing white even teeth – foreign teeth went through Julie's mind.

'I have been away on flying duties,' he said. 'I must explain. I am – was – Eileen's fiancé. We were engaged to be married—'

'Oh, my God!' Nancy gasped, sinking into a chair.

'It is a shock for you, I know,' he went on, 'and I am more sorry than I can say about – what happened. It was a tragedy. We were to have been married in September.'

Julie intervened before her mother could say anything.

'We knew nothing of this,' she said. 'Eileen lived very privately.'

'I know,' he said, but he gave her a look which showed her that he knew she had stayed in the flat.

She turned to Nancy. 'Mum, why don't you put the kettle on for tea? I'm sure Mr Szarnicki can do with a cup.'

Funny time for tea, Nancy thought – it was almost lunch-time. What was all this about?'

'Bob!' she called, while she waited for the kettle to

100

boil. 'You are never going to guess what's happened,' and she told him.

'How do you know he is speaking the truth? He might be a German spy.'

'I don't think he is,' she said slowly. 'Oh, Bob!' and she bit her lip to stop from crying.

'Hold on, Nan,' he said. 'Let's get to the bottom of this.'

'Well, young fella,' he said coming into the front room.

Josef got to his feet at once. 'Mr Halliwell—'

'Yes, that's me.'

Josef held out his hand. 'I am Josef Szarnicki, Eileen's fiancé.'

'Have you got something on you to prove who you are?' Bob asked.

Trust her dad to do the right thing, Julie thought, but she had no doubts herself, none at all. It was all falling into place.

'You've taken a long time to come and see us,' Bob said, glancing at his identity card.

'I am on flying duties, and based – well, I cannot tell you where – sufficient to say that I was not there when the bomb fell. I learned about it later. I have had to go to much trouble to find you. Eileen never told me where you lived, and there was nothing left – no record.' He turned away.

Poor man, Julie thought. How sad.

'I loved her very much,' he said.

To control her tears, Nancy went off to finish making the tea, and when she came back they were all in deep conversation.

'So you come from Poland and you're in the Polish Air Force, I take it. Where did you meet my daughter?'

'At the Servicemen's Club in South Kensington; she helped there. I had lost my wife two years before – she was killed in the bombing of Poland, and Eileen was very kind to me. Whenever I had leave, we shared it together, and soon after we became engaged. As I explained to your wife, we were to have been married in September.'

Nancy was openly weeping now.

'Don't upset yourself,' Bob said, patting her shoulder. 'It's nice to know that she had this young man.'

Josef went to his inside pocket and brought forth a tissue-wrapped photograph in an envelope. It was of himself and Eileen, his arm about her shoulders, Eileen laughing, as happy as they had ever seen her.

'Oh!' Nancy gasped. 'What a lovely picture of her! She looks so happy there – you both do.'

'It is my identification for you,' he said. 'I thought if you liked it, I – well, I brought you a present. If you had not been pleased I would not give it to you.'

He unwrapped another small packet containing a silver-framed photograph of the same picture.

'For us?' Nancy blinked.

'Of course,' he said.

'Oh, it's – lovely.'

As they sat and talked, Julie, choked with tears, went to carry on with the lunch. Undoubtedly they would ask him to stay – she would hope they did. What a nice young man, how awful that Eileen should have died as she did. It made her more certain than ever that you should grab life while you could.

'Please stay and have lunch with us,' Nancy said, wiping her eyes. 'Oh, I am glad you came.'

They need never know that Josef had lived at Eileen's flat; that would be her and Josef's secret, and she would never tell. The day had started off like any other day. Who would have thought such a thing possible as this young man turning up out of the blue? She didn't suppose they had seen the last of him. Bob seemed to like him. Imagine, she might have had a Polish brother-in-law . . .

He spent the afternoon with them and left promising to come and see them again, and Nancy didn't stop talking about it for a week. His visit occupied all her thoughts; she had nothing else on her mind, and every ten minutes her eyes would go to the mantelpiece where the silver-framed photograph sat.

How sad that Eileen had been so secretive, and all presumably because she hadn't wanted to upset her parents. But Julie realized that at the end of the day it was best to be open and above board. Her nineteenth birthday was approaching and she was about to tell them of Maurice's proposal. But strangely enough, Nancy forestalled her.

It was one evening in late August, and there was a sudden thunderstorm. The sky darkened over, and after the hot golden day, even the pavements steamed. Everything smelled fresh after the rain, the scents came up from Bob's flowers, and then the sun came out again brilliantly.

'What a lovely evening,' Nancy said. 'I wonder how they are getting on in Balmoral Street and who is getting the bombing tonight?' But without waiting for an answer, she put her sewing down, and looked at Julie.

'Julie, I've been thinking. You know that young man of Eileen's? Seeing him made such a difference, and I began to think, it's hard on you being up here, missing your friends . . .'

Julie was moved. 'Oh, Mum—'

'I think,' she said slowly, 'that you are very fond of this young man, Maurice. Am I right?' and Julie's cheeks burned.

'Yes I am, and he loves me too.'

'So I've gathered, by the post that comes, but after what happened to Eileen it seems to me that parents mustn't be selfish. You must do what you want to do, I can't hold you back; you're nearly nineteen now, and if that's what you want—'

'Oh, Mum!'

'Well, I don't say I approve, mind – I think he's far too old for you – but, well, why not ask him up to lunch one weekend? Would he come?'

'He's only waiting for the chance,' Julie laughed, and threw her arms around Nancy, something she was doing a lot, it seemed, since the war started . . .

So it was arranged that Maurice would come to Sunday lunch in two weeks' time, the first occasion when he would be free.

After helping to prepare lunch and lay the table, Julie went into York to meet Maurice's train. She saw him coming up the platform, fair hair glinting beneath his cap. He looked so handsome – what would her mother think of him?

He kissed her warmly, and Julie, taking his arm, made their way to the taxi rank, hoping there would be one available – it wasn't a foregone conclusion that one would, the war had changed all that.

However, they were lucky. Once in the taxi, he looked down at her, her slim figure showing off the bias-cut floral dress to perfection. The dark brows and lashes accentuated the blue eyes which shone especially for him, he was sure.

'I've been longing for this day to come,' he said. 'And I knew it would – some time.'

'You are very sure of yourself,' she squeezed his arm. 'I never thought it possible, but my mother has been wonderful, and so has Dad.'

The taxi stopped in front of the prefab, and when Julie unlocked the front door she found both her parents waiting there. If Nancy was overawed by this splendid handsome apparition, she didn't show it, while Bob held out his hand as if Maurice was an old friend.

Later, passing the hallstand with Maurice's peaked cap hanging there, Julie thought she must be dreaming.

Over lunch, which Nancy had taken time and trouble over, they talked of the war and living in York – everything but Julie's future. Only afterwards in the small sitting room did Bob take charge and put to Maurice the questions he had been formulating in his mind for the last few days.

'Well, Maurice,' he began. 'Julie tells me that you want to get married?'

'Yes, Mr Halliwell,' and looking at Julie, Maurice took her hand in his.

'I don't have to tell you that her mother and I have been worried, not just because of the age difference, but also because of the very different circumstances that exist. We don't like to think that you are both rushing into it because of the war. In normal times perhaps you wouldn't even consider such a thing. And Julie's background is very different from yours ...'

'I don't happen to believe in British so-called class distinction,' Maurice said. 'Nevertheless, I understand your anxiety. I need hardly tell you that I love her very much and will take care of her, rest assured of that.'

'Where will you live?' Nancy asked. 'I suppose you

would want to take her back to London?'

'Well, that is my base, but wherever I am sent, if that's possible. Otherwise Inverness Square.'

'What does your mother say?' Nancy interposed.

'She leaves me to make my own decisions,' Maurice said. 'She has met Julie, and is happy for me.'

They spent the rest of the afternoon discussing wedding plans and, when Maurice left, it had been decided that they would be married in York in November and hold a small reception in a nearby hotel, after which Maurice and Julie would leave for London.

But much water was to pass under the bridge before then . . .

In September a letter came from Gwen to tell them that she and Les Daly had been married in a register office a few days before.

'It was a very quiet affair,' Gwen wrote, 'because Les was due to go on a long mission and heaven knows when he will be back! There was no time to let you know, but I am so happy, and I wished you could have been there. I am still living in my parents' house but I would love to see you – I can't bear to think you are so far away. My mother is back from Devon. Love to you and your parents . . .'

'Well!' Nancy said when Julie showed her the letter. 'Little Gwen married – imagine – and to that Les Daly – well, I never!'

Julie had mixed feelings. Somehow she wasn't surprised; stranger things had happened in wartime – and she recalled their trips to the park and watching the boys play tennis. Well, she still had a soft spot for him – why shouldn't she. Loving Maurice as she did made no difference to the calf-love she had felt for Les Daly. She hoped he would be safe; the Navy in wartime was a very dangerous occupation.

She planned to go down to London and see Gwen as soon as she could. But fate had other things in store.

When a bomb dropped on Bob's factory in Yorkshire, it killed two of the night staff and razed the converted building to the ground. Hasty, temporary arrangements were made for the very important war work Bob's firm was doing, and it was decided to send the whole unit down to a remote part of Wales.

Nancy could hardly believe it. Bob was to leave within a week and there was no time to plan anything, even Julie's wedding. So amidst all the confusion, Bob left for Wales, while Nancy promised to follow him as soon as he could fix up a home for her.

'Perhaps it's all for the best,' she said, trying to look on the bright side. 'With you in London it won't make much difference whether your father and I are in Wales or in Yorkshire. But it's further away, isn't it? I shall never see you ...' and she looked so woebegone that Julie felt really sorry for her. It was hard at their age to be uprooted like this.

'Perhaps your Dad will be able to get back home for the wedding,' Nancy said.

'I certainly hope so,' Julie replied. 'I don't intend to get married without him.'

So with Maurice's first leave at the beginning of November, they were married one snowy, bitterly cold day in Yorkshire with one or two neighbours and Bob home from Wales on special leave. They had lunch at a small hotel in York and afterwards left on the train for London, Bob's arm around Nancy's shoulder, Nancy weeping and Julie starry-eyed.

'Oh, Bob,' Nancy said as they made their way out of the station. 'Do you think—'

'Too late now,' Bob said. 'What's done is done . . . Let's wish them all the best. Just the two of us now, Nan, and by the way, I've found a little place – small, for the two of us.'

'Oh, Bob,' she dried her eyes. 'Something to look forward to.'

Bloody war, thought Bob . . .

In the crowded train Julie sat close to Maurice, unable to believe that at last they were married, and she was Mrs de Gruyt. She thought she would never get used to it. It sounded so foreign. Meanwhile Maurice looked down at the young woman at his side vowing that he would do everything in his power to make her happy. She looked radiant, her light eyes glowing like sapphires beneath the pale blue hat atop the blonde curls, a single pink rose pinned to the front. Her complexion, he thought, was as fine as a baby's and he felt a moment's guilt shared by exultation that he was taking this English rose away from her family. Her pale blue suit fitted her perfectly, and she wore white doeskin gloves, a present from Nancy. On the long ride to King's Cross he held her hand, not caring that as an officer he was accountable.

He had booked rooms at the Hyde Park Hotel for two nights, knowing that once back in London they had to take their chances like anyone else. That was all the leave he had; he was due back at the War Office the next day, and Julie would find herself the only person in the tall house in Inverness Square. He would leave it to her to find a housekeeper or daily help – whatever she wanted, for his mother's housekeeper was staying with her down in Cornwall.

The taxi took them to the hotel and a porter showed them to their rooms. Julie had never stayed in an hotel before and was quite overcome by the splendour of it all, even in wartime. A maid hung her clothes after asking her what she would wear that evening and ran a bath which she stepped into gratefully, lying back in the scented water with the promise of soft white towels to come . . .

Her clothes were lying ready for her, pressed, her high-heeled shoes ready for her to step into. She slipped into the lacy suspender belt and satin camiknickers, and fine silk stockings, then the long cream silk dress with cap sleeves, and was adjusting the neckline when Maurice came in from the next room.

Going over to her, he put his arms around her and held her to him, kissing her long and deeply. Presently he withdrew from his pocket a long velvet box, and from it took a string of pearls. For all Julie knew, they might not be real, but when he had clasped them around her throat she knew by the creamy ivory of them against her skin that they were very fine pearls indeed.

She looked up at him, lips trembling. 'Oh, you are so good to me.' She put her arms around his neck pulling him down to her and kissing him while he held her close.

He broke away and she saw that he too was trembling slightly. 'I think we should be getting down to dinner. We have to make the most of every moment.'

'Darling Maurice,' she said, and picking up her wrap went with him to the lift.

Despite shortages of certain foods, the dinner was excellent, and when it was over they retired to their suite. When Maurice came out of the bathroom he saw her standing by the window in a long silk nightgown edged with lace. He put his arms around her, his head buried in the mane of hair which fell to her shoulders, then lifted her as though she were a doll and carried her over to the bed.

She looked up at him trustingly, and gave herself up to him. Nothing she had ever read had prepared her for such passion – she was shocked at first, and gave a little cry, but she was surprised at his gentleness with her, despite realizing that here was a man who desired physical love very strongly, and was not easily sated. She would get used to it in time, and was troubled by the slight disappointment she felt. She was happiest when he was holding her close and fondling her – perhaps, she thought on falling asleep exhausted, I am not a very sexy person. That was the word they used today. But she loved him with all her heart, dear, dear Maurice . . .

Chapter Nine

In the old days everyone knew one another in Inverness Square although they carefully guarded their privacy from outsiders. They were not all on visiting terms – there were those who were neighbours and those who were friends – but there was an innate cosiness about living in a square. A new resident left calling cards and, if confident of social status, awaited the return call; if perhaps not so confident, prayed that they would be accepted.

The war changed all that. Indeed, during the blitz, when people who could do so fled to safer places, houses in the Square could be bought cheaply enough for those who dared to take advantage of the price and brave the dangers of living in London during the raids. Two of the houses were let: one as a home for retired gentlewomen and the other as a home for unmarried mothers, which was the final straw for the area. The iron railings were removed for the war effort, the grass square with its beautiful plane trees now spawned an air-raid shelter, a deep one discreetly in keeping with the area – not for them the Anderson corrugated iron shelters above ground which were such a blot on the landscape. For a time, people could be seen hurrying across the narrow street and back again when the air-raid warning sounded, perhaps aided by a servant to see them across the narrow road, complete with blankets, the servant carrying food and drink. This died away after a time when the long so-called phoney war ended and people began to move away. It would be never the same again, they said. London would never be the same again.

By the time the real raids started there were still a few old residents left, but in Inverness Square rosebay, willow herb and mallow grew quickly round the shelter, shrubs had overgrown, several houses had been turned into flats – usually four or five to a house – and some houses had been boarded up and looked derelict. There were still a few which kept up appearances and among these was the de Gruyt residence, the long lease of which Maurice de Gruyt senior had had the sense to buy when he first came to London from Holland as a young man.

A taxi brought Maurice and Julie to No. 25 and, once inside, Julie looked round curiously. Fabulous paintings still hung on the walls, although sheets covered most of the furniture. It looked unlived-in and she remembered with horror the night she had stayed there in the basement and the terrible morning which followed . . .

Now she took off her coat and hat and hung them in the cloakroom, then stood looking round her.

'You haven't been living here since your mother left, Maurice?'

'No, I have a room at the War Office; sometimes I come home for the weekend if there's time, to check, that sort of thing. It's really rather late to talk this evening, you must be so tired, but I thought we would sleep in the spare room and then move into Mother's room when we have cleared it out.'

'But—'

'There has been so little chance to talk, and I ought to have explained before. Mother has decided to stay in Cornwall; there is no point, she says, at her age in coming back to London, and she is very happy there.'

To be mistress of this fine house was Julie's first thought. She had dreaded having a mother-in-law to overlook her.

'I have promised that we will go down to Mullion for the first free weekend. She is so looking forward to meeting you again – her successor, she says, to the House of de Gruyt.'

'Oh, Maurice, I do hope—'

'You'll be fine,' he said. 'I'm not going to like leaving you tomorrow morning, but I shall try to get home early, and we'll go out and find somewhere to eat. After all, we are on our honeymoon . . . Are you happy, Julie?'

'Blissfully,' she replied, not knowing if she was on her head or her heels.

Maurice left the next morning for the War Office, and Julie started by taking off the dust sheets everywhere and exploring the house. The old-fashioned kitchen was in the basement, the entrance hall and dining room on the ground floor, together with a cloakroom; on the next floor was a huge drawing room, or salon as Maurice called it, with a balcony overlooking the square, and a small spare room.

Maurice's mother's room was on the next floor, a large double room with a bathroom off it and a second bedroom, and upstairs two further bedrooms, presumably built as the maids' rooms.

And what a climb! Imagine the maids in the old days climbing all these stairs with trays and jugs of hot water – and they had no heating then . . .

Tying a voluminous apron around her (obviously one of Mrs Jones's) and a headscarf, Julie got to work.

She tackled the kitchen first, clearing out cupboards and the pantry, and then shopped for food. It was all so exciting to do for the first time as a newly married young woman. Of course, the house was much too large for them, but still, given time . . .

When Maurice arrived home there was a fire burning brightly in the dining room with wood and coal Julie had brought up from the cellar herself. She was used to doing that at home, but Maurice was shocked.

'Julie! You didn't carry that all the way up from the cellar!'

'Of course, why not?'

'Because you are my wife, and I won't have it! And what's this – the table laid – are we eating in?'

'Just something I bought locally: lamb chops, potatoes and cabbage, and fruit to follow. Lucky to find it, for there is a shortage of fresh fruit—'

He came over and took her in his arms. 'I just wonder if we have any champagne?' his eyes twinkled.

'Yes, I saw some down in the cellar,' she dimpled. 'After all, a housewife has to get to know her own store cupboard.'

He kissed her, then broke away. 'Now, I mustn't get side-tracked. I've got lots to talk to you about. But let me get the champagne first.'

When the cork had been popped and they sat drinking the sparkling wine, they both relaxed.

'It must seem very strange to you,' he said. 'I hope you will be happy here, and not too lonely.'

'I must find something to do, some work. What is happening about the business, Maurice?'

'Well, I have closed Church Street, at least for the

moment – and I have sent a lot of stuff into store. The lease runs out in ten years but I have decided to keep it as an art gallery.'

'Only as an art gallery?'

He nodded and her face fell. Paintings were not her strong point.

'But – and I hope you will like this – I am thinking of opening a small shop for fine art and antiques in Walton Street. I don't expect you know it?' She shook her head. 'Very exclusive, and the lease has just come up for sale. I have been enquiring about it. One could open it now, but the main thing is to secure it, then I thought perhaps you would work there, with an assistant, or manager. You haven't had quite enough experience to run it on your own yet but you'll learn. It's just a bad time. I wonder whether I could find someone to run it, an elderly man, perhaps, anyway, that's on my mind, and I wondered what you thought about it?'

'It sounds wonderful! Of course I should have to do something for the war effort, or I would be called up, wouldn't I?'

'As a young married woman they wouldn't call on you yet, but I daresay you would like to do something useful. Work in the Forces canteen or voluntary work.'

'Yes, I should like that.'

There was something in having an older husband, someone in charge, Julie thought, someone who hadn't still to make his way in the world. She was lucky . . .

'Anyway, with your approval, we'll go and look at Walton Street and size it up, and if we like it I'll deal with signing the lease.' He poured more champagne. 'I thought we would clear Mother's bedroom stuff, send down to Cornwall what she wants and then you can furnish it just as you want. Would you like that?'

'Oh, Maurice that would be wonderful. It's such a lovely room, overlooking the Square.'

'Well, that will keep you busy for a time, and I'll give you all the help I can when I'm free; I never know where I'm going to be sent.'

'What exactly do you do, Maurice?'

'Intelligence, mainly – but don't worry about that. I like to think I'm doing my bit, as it were.'

'Of course you are!'

'I suggest you start with ordering a new bed from Harrods – or do you want twin beds, Julie?' his deep blue eyes quizzed hers as she blushed.

'No, of course not.' She liked nothing more than cuddling up to Maurice, although twin beds were very fashionable.

'Good!' he said.

'And unless your mother wants them, I would like to keep some of the pieces. The furniture is so pretty . . .'

'Mainly French,' he said. 'And I expect she'll want her *bonheur du jour* – I said we would go down to Cornwall on the first couple of days I get free. You'll like it there – have you ever been there?'

'No,' Julie said, thinking she'd never been anywhere really, but he wouldn't understand that.

He came over to her, and tilted her chin. 'You're very young to take over all this responsibility, hardly out of the schoolroom.'

'Oh, Maurice, what nonsense!' She sprang to her own defence. She was a great deal tougher than the girls in Maurice's world. You had to be if you were brought up in Balmoral Street . . .

It was almost Christmas before Julie was fully organised in Inverness Square. Almost all the valuable paintings

116

had been sent away to be stored safely and the walls looked bare without them. She hung a few pictures from the top bedrooms and filled the house with cut flowers and leaves, and while Maurice was away she decided to go to see Gwen.

Everything looked so strange – there had been some slight damage to houses and there was a great crater in the road; the railings had gone and the gardens looked overgrown and pathetic. It all looked so ... war-torn, Julie decided, making her way to Gwen's house on this Saturday morning.

Gwen was delighted to see her – the same old Gwen yet different. They hugged each other and Gwen wept a little then both girls sat at the kitchen table and talked and talked.

'I want to know all about the wedding,' Julie said. 'You didn't send me any photographs.'

'Well, we didn't have many taken; it isn't as if we had a big white wedding, and I haven't got round to it yet, but this is the main one,' and there was Gwen in a light-coloured suit holding Les's arm as he looked down at her. It seemed so strange to see them together. She was carrying roses and wore a perky hat on her dark hair.

'You look lovely, Gwen,' Julie said, and she meant it. They looked so well suited – made for each other, you might say, Gwen so dark and Les so fair.

'I hope you brought one for me,' Gwen said. 'Funny to think I've never even met the man you've married.'

Julie withdrew the postcard-size picture of her wedding, looking composed at Maurice's side, Maurice in uniform. She was aware how much older he appeared than Les Daly.

'Oh,' said Gwen dubiously, 'he's very good-looking, but so much older than you. Are you happy, Julie?'

'Very,' Julie smiled.

'Did you mind – I mean – were you upset when you heard I was going to marry Les?' and wondered as she had many times before if Julie had been caught on the rebound.

Julie laughed. 'Upset? Oh, of course not, Gwen,' and hugged her. 'I admit I was a little surprised because I thought you liked Martin.'

'Never saw him again,' Gwen said seriously.

'So you had to make do with Les!' And they laughed and giggled. It was just like old times.

'You've changed a bit,' Gwen said looking at her.

'Have I? How?'

'I can't put my finger on it exactly, but I suppose we both have. We're married women now.'

She got up to put the kettle on. 'Tell me all about where you live; after all, your life has changed more than somewhat, while mine, well mine stays just the same.'

'Yes, that's true. I'm hoping you will come and see us in Inverness Square – any time, Gwen – Maurice is away quite a bit anyway, but any time you can fit it in, we'd just love to see you.'

'Oh, I will,' Gwen assured her.

'Where are your mother and your little brother?'

'She's taken him shopping, but they'll be back for lunch – she's looking forward to seeing you, Julie.'

Lunch passed off pleasantly enough, with Gwen's mother obviously proud of her daughter's marriage and frowning slightly at the picture of Julie and her new husband.

She made no comment except to ask after Julie's parents, shocked when she heard they had been moved yet again, to Wales.

'Poor things,' she said. 'Losing a daughter like that

and now you moving away. London, is it?'

She was a miserable woman, Julie decided; she had never liked her anyway.

She was sorry to leave Gwen though, and thought about her on the journey back to Charing Cross, and how much she missed her.

Maurice was unexpectedly home when she arrived back in Inverness Square and looked so pleased to see her, she fell into his arms.

'I missed you,' he said. 'It is the first time I have come back to an empty house since we were married.'

There was no doubt about his love for her, she thought, looking up at him – the way his hair wanted to curl despite being slicked back, the blue eyes looking at her now as if he would never let her go. They were lucky, she told herself, to be together, even though he went away quite often. Imagine poor Gwen, always worried in case anything happened to Les. Life on a minesweeper must be hell . . .

One cold March morning they took the train to Cornwall to visit Maurice's mother. The train was full; they had difficulty in finding registrations, but armed with a gift of flowers Julie found herself looking forward to the journey. She wore a tweed skirt with a matching long coat and a fur collar, and a perky Tyrolean velour hat with a feather at the side.

Mrs de Gruyt had sent the taxi to meet them from Mullion Cove, and now it drew up outside the pretty little cottage which was surrounded by daffodils coming out so much earlier in this part of the world.

'Oh, it's lovely to see you both!' his mother cried. Julie could not have wished for a warmer welcome. Mrs de Gruyt obviously approved of her appearance, and

119

recalled that they had not seen each other since that fateful night of the bombing.

'Ah, here is Mrs Jones; we have both been very excited about your coming, my dear, we live very quiet lives down here. Are these for me? Oh, thank you! Roses at this time of year!'

It got dark quite quickly and pulling the curtains in the cottage living room Mrs Jones showed them upstairs to Mr Maurice's room, as she called it.

'I have to say, I feel quite guilty at bringing a girl up here,' Maurice grinned as Julie hung her things in the wardrobe. 'It's always been my room – we've been coming here since I was a small boy.'

'I'll go if you like,' she said swiftly, but Maurice caught her to him.

'Don't you dare!'

'Now, Maurice, you must tell me all your plans, ' his mother said as they sat with a glass of sherry before dinner.

And Maurice repeated them to his mother, who listened carefully.

'Firstly, we would like to know what you would like sent down here, because we will be making some changes in Inverness Square. Not major ones until after the war, but for the immediate future.'

They discussed this at some length before Maurice told her of his idea to turn the Church Street premises into an art gallery and his interest in the Walton Street lease.

'Certainly sounds a good plan, except that your timing is not very good. Have you seen the shop?'

'I know where it is, a nice little place. I thought Julie and I would go to look at it at the first opportunity.'

'And what do you think about it, Julie? Does it appeal to you?'

'Oh, I have to leave the business side of things to Maurice. I am still a novice.'

'Yes, my dear, but it is your life too, and as far as you can you must plan for the future. Would you be happy to work in the shop?'

'Yes, if Maurice thought I was knowledgeable enough, but as he explained, he would get someone in to manage it until I became more experienced.'

'And when a young couple plan for the future they have to take into consideration a coming family,' Mrs de Gruyt said mildly.

Julie's cheeks flushed, and even Maurice looked a little disconcerted. 'Yes, well, Mother—' he began. 'There's plenty of time for a family. We certainly wouldn't want one in wartime, would we, Julie?' and he took her hand.

'Babies, seldom if ever, choose the right time,' his mother said.

Julie was given a bunch of early daffodils to take back to London, and Mrs de Gruyt kissed her warmly on leaving.

'Now you must do whatever you like at Inverness Square. I hand it over to you with my blessing and I hope you will be as happy there as I have been; it's a lovely old house.'

'I love it already,' Julie said truthfully.

In May they went to see the premises in Walton Street and Julie was more than impressed, full of excitement at the prospect of opening an antique shop there, while Maurice began negotiations to buy the lease and to look around for someone to run the shop for him with help from Julie. Yes, it wasn't a good time, but the war wouldn't last for ever he told himself.

He was away a good deal that year, never saying where he had been, but Julie knew that he had been abroad quite a few times. It was a lonely life, but she worked at the Forces canteen and spent every spare moment learning from Maurice's vast collection of books on antiques and art. One weekend when the bombing had been particularly heavy, she went to Wales to spend a day or two with her parents and was pleased to find them happily settled in. They had a small house in a row of terraced houses, and lots of friendly neighbours; it was more like Balmoral Street than Yorkshire, Nancy said.

She made he way home knowing that they were in the best place, and returned to more bombing attacks. She moved herself down to the basement, climbing back up the stairs to daylight when the 'All clear' sounded. Every day she headed to the Forces canteen for morning duty, and spent three or four afternoons a week helping at the Citizen's Advice Bureau. It was a strange life, but so were most people's lives these days.

She got to know some of the people in the Square, residents who had been there since before the war and were determined to stay put. There were the Redmonds, a titled family whose only daughter, Elaine, did nothing to uphold the name of her famous politician father, but who drove an ambulance and served in the Red Cross. The Forrest family who lived next door but now consisted of Blake Forrest and his wife Sybil, who had an antique shop in the King's Road in Chelsea. Blake's parents were both dead and had left him the house in Inverness Square. Blake was about forty and there seemed to be no question of his going into the Forces. He and Sybil left each day to go to the King's Road, and often went to auctions which seemed to be more popular than ever now that people were moving house from one end of the country to the other or being bombed out. Julie had met them once or twice when Maurice was at home and they had had them round for drinks. She got on quite well with Sybil Forrest, but was not too sure about Blake. He had eyed her with open admiration and held her hand a little too long when they were introduced. She still was not too sure of herself in this new world except on the business side.

Then Gwen came for the weekend. Excited at the prospect of seeing her, Julie met her at the station and they walked back to Inverness Square.

'Here?' she asked as Julie unlocked the front door and let her in. 'Golly – it's enormous!' although she had somehow imagined it surrounded by gardens. Julie made coffee and took it up to the drawing room.

'What a lovely view. Seems funny, though, to go upstairs to the sitting room; don't you get lonely here by yourself?'

'Sometimes,' Julie said. 'I'll show you upstairs after we've had our coffee. Now tell me how you've been getting on. I thought we'd go out to Fortnum's for lunch – how does that sound?' aware that she sounded slightly condescending.

'Lovely,' Gwen said. 'I'm just enjoying myself. It makes such a change from being at home with Mum. You know what she is like.'

'Well, you'll have a place of your own after the war,' Julie said. 'Won't it be wonderful when it ends? I can't imagine it.'

'Nor me. Les has been gone three months now – I've almost forgotten what he looks like!'

They went out to dinner and sat up until nearly

midnight chatting over old times. The next day they went for a walk in Hyde Park and Kensington Gardens and after lunch Gwen prepared to go home.

'I can't imagine you living up here among all these old things – antiques – but you've always liked old things, haven't you? You went mad when you worked in that funny little shop, do you remember?' and they laughed.

'When I get a home of my own, I'm going to have the most modern furniture I can find – Les has promised me – a limed oak dining room suite and a sideboard fitted out as a cocktail cabinet. Well, it's still sitting in Chiesman's window – I expect it will be gone by the time I want it!'

'Oh, I know what I've forgotten – won't be a tick.' Julie flew upstairs and came down with a small package, something wrapped in tissue paper, and handed it to her. 'It just takes a single rose,' Julie said. 'And here's the date underneath: London hallmark eighteen twenty-six.' But she could see it meant nothing to Gwen.

'Oh, it's sweet!' Gwen said – 'but you shouldn't have. Thanks, Julie. Well, I must be on my way. I must say, you are lucky living here, with a husband who adores you.' Gwen looked quite wistful.

'Come on, cheer up. Les'll be home soon, and Maurice, too, I hope.'

I'd like to meet him, he sounds nice,' Gwen said.

Towards the end of the year Maurice came home, travel-stained and tired. There was still sporadic bombing, some very heavy attacks, but he was glad to be home and would say nothing about where he had been.

'I'll tell you one day – after the war.' His eyes looked tired and red-rimmed and he had lost weight.

Julie insisted that he should go straight to bed after a

124

hot bath, and rest there for a couple of days.

That night was one of the worst raids in the war, but Maurice insisted on staying in his bed.

'I've got a week's leave and I'm not spending it in the basement,' he said.

The following day they learned that a direct hit had demolished Blake and Sybil's premises in the King's Road.

'Poor devil!' Maurice said when he heard, but after a few moments he sat up straight, a gleam in his eye.

'Just a thought,' he said.

Chapter Ten

'Oh, Maurice, you wouldn't!' Julie cried.

'Why not?' Maurice's eyes were alight with enthusiasm. 'Look, darling, here's Blake with his business razed to the ground, he's lost his shop and his stock – what better man to take over the managership of Walton Street? Of course, he may not be interested, I understand that, but he's got to be doing something – he's an expert in the trade. But—' Maurice could see the doubt in Julie's eyes. 'You don't like him?' He was puzzled. How could she admit that she did not dislike Blake Forrest as much as mistrust him – and she had nothing to go on, not really.

'It isn't that, Maurice, but if I'm to work in the shop I'm not sure I'd get on with Blake. He's not the slightest bit like you.'

'Perhaps that's just as well,' he laughed. 'Anyway, what am I saying, he may not be interested, but it occurred to me as an idea.'

'Then if you think so,' Julie said doubtfully. 'I'm not qualified to interfere, really. I'm still a new girl.'

He came over and took her in his arms. 'And a beautiful new girl, at that,' he said. 'Well, we'll see. I'll mention it to Blake, sound him out.'

And Julie had to be content with that for the time being.

The shop lease was duly signed; they were to take over in October. And what about Sybil, Julie wondered. She and Blake ran the King's Road shop together – nothing was turning out as she had imagined.

Maurice was away for the next two weeks and when he returned suggested to Julie that they ask Blake and Sybil round to dinner. Julie agreed – she would like the opportunity to get to know Sybil better, she had always admired her.

Julie had prepared everything in the dining room, hoping that there would not be a raid, or at least not a heavy one, and when the doorbell rang heard Maurice go to answer it. She went forward to meet them and saw at once that they were both under great strain.

'Come in,' Maurice said. 'It's nice to see you. We thought you might like a bit of cheering up after the disaster.'

'You can say that again,' Blake said morosely. 'If only we hadn't kept so much bloody stuff in the shop. Sorry Julie.'

'Sit down, make yourselves comfortable,' she said, seeing how Sybil's rather nice brown eyes looked so sad now, her eyebrows drawn together anxiously.

'Very nice of you, Julie,' she said. 'Just the sort of break we can do with,' and she turned to Blake who smiled at her and patted her arm.

'What will you have: wine, whisky, sherry?'

'A dry sherry for me, please,' Sybil said.

'And a whisky for me,' Blake said.

When they were all comfortably settled with drinks, Maurice toasted them. 'Here's to the end of the war and

127

lasting peace,' he said. 'As a matter of fact I do have another reason for asking you here this evening.'

'Ah, I thought there was a catch in it,' Blake said; his eyes were wary. 'Are you going to tell us now?'

'Yes, might as well. I've taken the lease out on a shop in Walton Street.'

'You what?' Blake almost shouted in disbelief.

'Yes, sounds a little mad, doesn't it, at this particular time, but the opportunity was there, and I took it. I've signed up and we open in October.'

'Well, rather you than me,' Blake said.

'You don't rate my chances?'

'I should say not!'

'Well, the deed's done now, but here's what I've been thinking: what are you going to do now your shop's been busted?'

'Me? Well, not much I can do until after the war.'

'The idea occurred to me that you might be prepared to go into the Walton Street shop as manager. It would be a temporary arrangement of course, and you would be free to leave any time you liked if it didn't suit.'

'Suppose I get called up, I'm forty-seven.'

'Not very likely, is it? And you do your Home Guard stint. But how do you feel about the actual job?'

'Tell me what you're thinking,' Blake said, looking serious. 'Stock – that sort of thing.'

'The usual. Small pieces of furniture: you see, I've decided after the war to turn Church Street into a paintings-only gallery – an art gallery, in effect – and Walton Street would take care of the bric-à-brac, porcelain, that sort of thing. Get the idea?'

'I'm staggered,' Blake said, 'to put it bluntly. What do you think, Julie?'

'Oh, she would work there too.' Blake's eyes lit up.

'Oh, well, then, in that case, I accept!'

Sybil gave him a little push. 'Behave yourself, Blake,' she smiled, but her eyes weren't smiling, Julie noticed.

Maurice put his arm round Julie. 'This young lady shows a lot of promise – knows something nice when she sees it – so I want her to get as much experience as she can.'

Seeing the look Blake gave her, Julie stood up. 'I think the meal is almost ready. It's quite simple, nothing fancy. I'll give you a shout.'

While they sat around the table, Maurice expounded his theory that when matters were at their worst was the time to chance something, and take the bull by the horns. His father had done a similar thing in the First World War.

'Well, it's a new theory to me, but I'll go for it,' Blake said, helping himself to hors d'oeuvres. 'After all, it's your money.'

'We'd have to discuss salary, commission, that sort of thing. The shop will be re-decorated by October and we hope it will be stocked and ready by the first of November.'

'Just right for the Christmas trade,' Blake said. 'You hope!'

'I never knew you were such a defeatist,' Maurice said.

'You might be if you'd just had the experience of being bombed out,' Blake said grimly.

Sybil's soft voice interrupted them. 'What about me? What am I supposed to be doing while all this activity is taking place in Walton Street? I've always worked in the shop, and there's no way I want to do war work or go into a factory.'

'You could work part time,' Maurice said. 'Be

company for Julie.'

Julie did hope so. The more she saw of Blake Forrest the less she liked the idea of working with him. 'Oh, that's a wonderful idea!' she cried. 'How about it, Sybil?'

'You expect to be making a lot of money in this new venture then?' Blake asked with sarcasm.

'Why not?' Maurice asked as he watched Julie serve out the casserole. 'Help yourselves to vegetables, do.'

'Smells simply delicious,' Sybil said. 'It's lovely not having to cook.'

Julie looked at her gratefully.

It was nearly midnight when the Forrests left, and Maurice was so pleased with the turn of events that he was like a dog with two tails.

'There, I told you it would work out,' he said as they went upstairs to bed.

The decoration of the shop with its new fascia, THE HOUSE OF DE GRUYT, was finished halfway through October, fine brass grilles to deflect bomb blast and specially plated windows. Then, with Maurice away, she and Blake and Sybil went down to the safe bomb-proof hideaway where a lot of the stock was stored, and marked off what they would take to furnish the shop. Later Blake hired a van to collect it and Julie made a special journey up north to the secret vaults where most of the porcelain and fine art was kept. It was becoming really exciting.

At this time the Germans were busy holding on to their invasion of Russia, while in North Africa Rommel and his men were slowly but surely being defeated. At least there was a lull in the bombing of Britain; Germany and

Italy were otherwise occupied and with a sudden lifting of spirits Julie busied herself stocking up the Walton Street shop.

The walls were covered in rich ruby red damask. Maurice had insisted that no expense be spared, they must start off in the right direction. A lot of stock was put in the empty rooms upstairs and the smaller pieces arranged carefully; the walls were hung with small pictures, most of the stuff from Maurice's old shop in Church Street. The gilt frames stood out against the crimson walls, and magnificent crystal candelabra, which shone like diamonds under electric light, hung from the ceilings.

'I think he's mad,' Blake said.

The shop was filled with flowers for the opening day. It might have been peacetime for all it mattered, and Julie in a new outfit bought with her precious clothing coupons, a new hairdo, her nails tinted rosy red, her high heels clacking on the parquet floor, busied herself with last-minute touches. This wasn't south London, she told herself, but the centre of the metropolis, war or no war. Blake, handsome and immaculate, busied himself at the small desk, while Sybil was a discreet figure in the background.

It made quite an impact locally, and there were many window-shoppers. People seemed to like the touch of luxury the salon gave to the area.

By the end of the week they had sold two pieces of fine furniture, and several pieces of porcelain. It seemed a shame, thought Julie, that the blackout shutters had to come down every evening so that the contents of the shop window were hidden from passers-by.

As Christmas drew near and sales became better, Julie

noticed that whenever Sybil was in the shop Blake behaved perfectly. She usually came in three days a week. But whenever she was not there Blake's tactics changed. If he could brush by Julie closely, he would. Wanting information, he would take her arm and ask her confidentially. Julie was not surprised. She had always known that Blake would be like this, and felt sorry for Sybil. She could more than cope with Blake whom she disliked more than ever, but consoled herself with the fact that soon Maurice would be home on a spot of leave.

She had a Christmas card from Gwen saying that she and her father were going to join her mother and brother in Devon for the festive season. At the first opportunity she was going to come up to London to see the new venture. While it was quiet Maurice's mother, escorted by Mrs Jones, made one of her rare visits to London, and they all spent Christmas Day at the Knightsbridge Hotel. On the way back home they visited the new shop and were very impressed.

Maurice was not due to return to the War Office until the New Year, and it was on January the first that Julie received the telephone call.

'For you, Julie,' he said.

'Who is it?'

'I didn't quite get his name,' Maurice said, and Julie's first thought was of her parents.

'Hello?'

'Julie?' she didn't recognise the voice.

'It's Les – Les Daly—' the voice said, and she knew immediately that something was wrong.

'Les!'

'I'm afraid I have some bad news for you.'

But she almost knew what it was before he told her.

'It's Gwen. I'm sorry to bring you such bad news,

Julie, but Gwen – she's dead. Killed in a car accident.'

'Oh no!' She stifled her cry. 'How?'

'She was in a taxi with her mother and brother on her way to the station to come home when an ambulance rushing to an alarm after a bomb alert collided with them. Her mother and young Teddie were thrown out, but Gwen—' and his voice broke.

'Oh,' Julie whispered. 'Oh, Les, I am sorry.' She tried to hold back the tears, her throat hurt so. 'Was she killed instantly?' She couldn't bear to think of Gwen suffering.

'Yes, her neck was broken.'

'Oh, Les! When is the funeral?'

'Here, next Tuesday.'

'I'll be there,' she said.

'You'll come?' he said. He sounded surprised.

'Just tell me when and where.'

'St Luke's Church, two-thirty. Look, Julie—'

'I'll be there, Les,' she said, and, putting down the telephone, burst into tears.

Maurice took her in his arms. 'I heard,' he said. 'Oh, darling, I am so sorry. For such a thing to happen – please don't upset yourself . . .'

But she sobbed as if her heart would break. 'We've known each other since we were five,' she said.

'When is the funeral?'

She dried her eyes, 'Next Tuesday.'

'Would you like me to come with you?'

'No thank you, Maurice, I'd rather go alone. Can you manage?'

'Of course,' he said.

It was a wretched journey across London; the air-raid warning went twice, but nothing happened and, taking a taxi from the station to St Luke's Church, her eyes filled with tears as she walked up the path – the path that she and

133

Gwen had walked up so many times on a Sunday. The organ was playing softly; a young man handed her the Order of Service and she took her seat in one of the pews at the back until she could accustom herself to the dark interior.

Everyone was in black; she could see Les at the front, Gwen's mother and father, her brother and possibly a few relatives. She still couldn't believe it was real and she could hardly bear to look at the coffin, which was covered with white flowers.

There were no more than twenty people there and Julie was really glad she had come. The hymns were sad and the eulogy brief for Gwen had had such a short life.

Julie walked outside into the brilliant winter sunshine, and saw the wreaths, her own of bright yellow daffodils, for Gwen who had come from Wales. Gwen's parents hardly noticed her as they passed, but Les, in black, came straight over to her and took her arm.

'Julie, thank you for coming.'

Round the graveside on this bitterly cold morning Julie, in her black coat and hat, listened in wonder. This couldn't be happening. She felt she wanted to leave at once, but knew she must stay. Everyone would be going back to Gwen's home – it was the least she could do.

It was a sorry gathering. Mr and Mrs Edwards came over to have a word with her, but, like her, they must have felt as if they were in a dream or a nightmare. Les and the family were kept busy, and Julie felt it was time she took her leave. Mrs Edwards thanked her for coming, and kissed her briefly on the cheek.

'Goodbye, my dear.'

'I'll give you a lift to the station,' Les said.

In the car beside him, Julie felt his proximity and wondered how it could be that here she was sitting next to the boy she had fallen in love with a few years ago.

They talked perfunctorily of this and that on the short journey, and he parked the car outside the station and saw her to the station foyer.

'I am so sorry, Les,' Julie said, now too upset to even weep. He was close to weeping himself and she guessed that he had been bottling up his feelings throughout the day. Suddenly he put his arms round her and held her close to him. 'Oh, Julie, I don't know how I'm going to live without her.' They heard the train coming and he released her.

'I'll write,' she called, almost blinded by tears as she fled down the station steps to the platform; but she knew she wouldn't. A soldier stood up to allow her to sit down and she huddled into the corner. It could have been anyone, she told herself, a stranger. To think I would have given my right arm to be held in Les's arms at one time, but now it meant nothing. For years he was my idol; did I imagine it all? For it wasn't loyalty to Gwen – she knew that. Trying to take her mind off the actual funeral she thought of the doubts she had had about Maurice. Was she really in love with Les? Her disappointment at the physical side of marriage – had she been hoping it was Les? The fierce feeling of jealousy when she heard Gwen was going to marry him. Her doubts that perhaps she was in love with Maurice's world, his fine standard of living after life in Balmoral Street – was she exchanging the dross for the gold? 'Did you mind,' Gwen had asked her, 'when you knew I was going to marry Les?' – and she had laughed – 'Good Lord, no!' But she had.

And now Les is free, she thought, and I feel nothing – nothing but sorrow for Gwen who had to die so soon . . .

She let herself into the house and found Maurice sitting by the fire. He got up and hurried over to her. She flung herself into his arms, so thankful to be home, for the first time feeling the freedom of loving someone wholeheartedly. He kissed her gently, then held her against him, feeling her fast-beating heart next to his own. He made no effort to ask her how she had got on – he could tell how glad she was to be home again and they stayed like that, he holding her and looking over her head but unseeing.

'I love you so much, Maurice,' she said at length.

'I know you do,' he said.

Chapter Eleven

It was some months before the war ended that Maurice de Gruyt was given his discharge from the War Office. Only then did Julie learn that her clever husband spoke four languages fluently and that he had been working for a long time at Bletchley Park in Buckinghamshire where some of the most important work in the war had been carried out, trying to break the German codes. Some of the finest brains in the country had been working there, and now it was beginning to pay off, for there was a distinct feeling in the air that peace could not be far away. With the brilliant strategy of the combined war leaders and the bravery of the Armed Forces people told themselves it could not be long now.

It was wonderful to have Maurice home, and the first week they went down to Cornwall to see old Mrs de Gruyt, who had been unwell of late. Her devoted companion–housekeeper, Mrs Jones, had been worried about her and was delighted to see Maurice and his beautiful young wife. They went for long walks in the countryside where even now in February the daffodils were beginning to show their long spears, the birds were singing and there was a message of hope in the air.

Julie had never been happier. The air was fresh and clean after the thick atmosphere or wartime London, air which was clogged with the dust of debris, smoke and bomb blast, and they made the most of their time there.

Maurice had misgivings about his mother and told Julie that he doubted whether she would last long enough for another visit. She had had a long life and now a heart condition, and Mrs Jones confided to them that Mrs de Gruyt had wanted to live long enough to see the war come to an end, then she would be quite happy to depart this life – besides, she was curious to know what lay on the other side. She covered Maurice's hands with hers. 'What will you do now, Maurice?' she asked.

'After this wonderful break, I shall return to Walton Street with Julie to take up the reins again.'

'What will happen to the Forrests?' For Mrs de Gruyt knew them well, having known Blake's father.

'Oh, Blake knew it was only a temporary thing. In any case, he and Sybil are planning to open their own place again, or will as soon as the war is over.'

'Remember me to him, I recall him so well as a little boy. He was so naughty – the plague of his father's life – but he grew up to be so good-looking, such a handsome man.'

'Still is,' laughed Maurice and looked towards Julie for confirmation, but she only smiled.

'Now, you look after yourself until we come down again and do as Mrs Jones tells you. I'll be in touch. Call me if there is anything you need.'

'It was great seeing her again,' he told Julie on the train 'but I don't like the look of her.'

Julie took his hand in hers. 'Don't worry darling ... Oh, I am so glad to have you home again,' she said. 'Now we can really start our new life together.'

When the Allies advanced into Germany there was no doubt that peace was on its way; Hitler committed suicide in April and on 7 May Germany surrendered. The European war was over.

The country went mad before it settled down again to peace having paid the high price of the horrendous years which had taken such a toll on life and brought such misery and unhappiness to so many people.

The de Gruyts counted themselves fortunate. They were able to pick up the pieces and put together their business. Maurice was to work in the Walton Street shop while he looked at the possibilities of reopening the Church Street gallery.

One late afternoon in June when Maurice had gone to a house sale in Bath, Julie sat at her desk going through the accounts. Blake had left early to keep a business appointment while Sybil had gone to see her mother in Richmond. They had stayed on in the shop until Maurice had got his gallery business settled and had sorted out the lease of the Church Street premises.

Presently the door pushed open and a customer came in, a man of swarthy Middle Eastern appearance whom she recognized as a new neighbour in Inverness Square.

Greeting him, he bowed his head slightly, recognizing her and betraying his interest in a rather nice piece of furniture, a French commode. Julie explained its provenance to him as he bent to examine it, fingering the patina of the wood, the shape of the legs, the design on the front. He seemed to have no doubt at all that he wanted it, but she was used by now to the different ways in which foreigners purchased goods. Some took hours to to decide – days, even – but this man knew what he wanted.

'I will have it,' he said, his large dark eyes almost black with concealed excitement at the prospect of owning yet another precious work of art.

They stood looking at the French commode, Aristide Ionides and Julie de Gruyt. Sometimes it seemed to him that everything in the UK was for sale if one only asked. Whatever – a house, a horse, a piece of fine art. 'You wish to sell?' you would ask, and often they would answer. 'At a price . . .'

He was reminded of his grandfather telling him that the old Queen Mary (his grandfather had been educated at Eton and knew Queen Mary personally), on her rounds often admired objects, and whatever she admired, she was given. But this was different. This lady, Madame de Gruyt, charming as she was, was a neighbour whom he happened to have met on a social occasion, and he was intrigued, especially when he learned that she had an antique and fine art gallery in Walton Street. Well, he wasn't like Queen Mary, he was prepared to pay the full asking price, which he suspected was quite over the top, but business was business, and this delightful lady was prepared to sell.

'Yes, Madame,' he said. 'I will have it. You will deliver it for me next week?'

'Yes, of course, Mr Ionides,' Julie said. 'At a time to suit you, of course.'

'Any time. There are always plenty of people there to take it in.'

Too true, Julie thought.

He bowed slightly, and turned to the little figure who had followed him in. Silent in all this time, a tiny lady dressed in black wearing a yashmak who had waited patiently; perhaps she was his wife, there was no way of knowing, but her perfume filled the salon.

The small scented creature stood aside for him to leave and he moved ahead of her, while she followed.

'Good afternoon, Madame.'

'Good afternoon, Mr Ionides.'

I suppose he will follow this up with a cheque when I submit my bill, thought Julie. Well, he is a new neighbour, and he will certainly not get the commode until he has paid for it. She was always shocked, though no longer surprised, at the way some people behaved over money; the more wealthy they were, the more disinclined they were to part with their money.

She would be sorry to see the commode go, it was one of her favourite pieces, but business was business, and expensive though it was, it was worth every penny they had asked for it. Who knew what its value would be in the future?

It had been a warm, humid, sticky sort of day for June, thunder-clouds about and a lowering sky, but the threatened rain never arrived and around five-thirty the skies cleared and somewhat surprisingly the sun came out.

In the premises of the House of de Gruyt in Walton Street, Julie sat back in the inner office and glanced at her watch, checking with the large Louis XIV clock on the wall, and decided it was time to close shop for the day. She stood for a moment or two, looking around the salon, the colours of the curtains were lit by shafts of sunlight and the elegant lamps would light up the dark silks of the well-chosen furnishings. The walls were covered with dark red silk and there were oil paintings enough to bring a tear to the eye of any art collector who might be passing. Of course, the security was great and cost the earth but always when closed the grilles came down thus ensuring safety while enabling the viewer to enjoy the display. The House of de Gruyt accepted that the cost of insurance alone made great inroads into profits, but also knew that many a sale had been made from prospective purchasers looking in the windows while taking an evening stroll or walking a dog after dark.

141

Maurice's father, the first Maurice de Gruyt, had prospered, his knowledge being extensive, and he was respected and known throughout the art world.

Julie loved the small gallery. In one corner stood a white marble figure of Aphrodite, in another a large golden cage which held colourful exotic birds, examples of the taxidermist's art. In the centre the figure of a young girl of great beauty stood dressed in the clothes of the court of Marie Antoinette.

Here and there one glimpsed a piece of Sèvres, an example of the Frenchman's art with porcelain; there was English silver displayed on red velvet, a delicate rosewood table, and in one corner a fall of red silk tartan draped back with a huge royal blue bow.

Julie's mouth softened into a smile as she thought of her husband driving back from Bath where he had been to a house sale, and wondered if he had been able to secure the painting he wanted.

Raising her arms, she stretched to relax, then went round checking the various alarm systems and, picking up her handbag, with one last look behind her, carefully locked the door. Once outside, she decided to walk home on this fine evening instead of calling a taxi, and made for the de Gruyt family home in Inverness Square.

She inserted her key in the lock and opened the door which led to the hall and the sitting room and the kitchen. The basement was in darkness which meant that the daily help would have gone home as she usually did on a Friday after lunch.

Julie bathed and changed into silk pyjamas and a loose housecoat, trying it around her waist. Time to relax; she put on the radio to listen to soft music. There was no meal to prepare – perhaps they would go out to dinner. It would depend what time Maurice got back. She helped herself to a glass of wine thinking about the large commission she had received this week from a young American woman who had bought a flat in Knightsbridge, and spent a small fortune on antiques with which to furnish it.

She was startled by the ring of the front doorbell and hurried to answer it.

'Who is it?' she called through the door.

'Julie, it's me, Blake,' came the distorted tones.

Blake Forrest ... frowning, she glanced down at herself; she was more respectably dressed than if she had been in the street.

'Oh, Blake, hello.' She undid the safety chain.

The door opened and Blake came in, grinning as he kissed her lightly on the cheek. Julie wondered why he was alone. Perhaps Sybil wasn't back yet from Richmond.

'Come in and sit down. Maurice is on his way back from Bath; he'll be here soon.' She wondered why she had to stress that, but there was something a little unsettling about Blake, suave and charming as he was – you were never quite sure. Not that he had ever put a foot wrong.

'What would you like, Blake? A drink? Coffee?' Have you eaten?' She had no intention of telling him she did not expect Maurice for an hour or more.

He sat down on the sofa in his elegant pale sweater and tweed jacket, slim-fitting trousers, his expensive shoes well polished, his eyes roguishly smiling into hers.

'I shouldn't mind a glass of wine to begin with,' he said. 'I rather wondered if you might like to go out for a meal – Syb won't be back until late.'

'I'll get us some wine,' she said.

Going over to the cabinet to pour, she realized that she wished he hadn't come to spoil her nice quiet siesta.

'Here we are,' she said, going over to him and placing his glass on the side table. 'Have some olives, nuts, whatever.'

'Thanks,' he said, diving into the bowls. 'How's life with you then – how did you get on today?'

'Great,' she said, taking a sip. 'Business is surprisingly good. I sold the French commode.'

'Lucky you,' he said and held up his glass. 'Well, here's to success.'

She smiled back at him, lifting her glass. He really was a handsome devil, but there was something about him – why was it that you felt you couldn't trust him?

'And how are things with you? Have you been over to Paris lately? I hear there was a wonderful château sale?'

'Yes, I went. Sybil's not bothered.' Julie wondered about them. She had an idea that Sybil spread her favours around, in which case he must have a hard time. No wonder she sometimes caught a discontented expression on his face.

'Look, are you hungry?' she asked. 'I could rustle up a snack. I had lunch out today.'

'Yes, thanks, that would be nice.'

'Paté, ham, cheese, fruit.'

'Excellent,' he said, going over to the cabinet and helping himself to more wine. Then he sat back on the sofa, stretching his long legs out in front him, relaxed.

After more idle talk, Julie made her way to the kitchen where she found the bread, butter and cheeses and was piling the tray when she heard a swift movement behind her and suddenly felt two arms steal around her waist and hold her in a strong grip.

'Blake!' She wrestled with him. 'What on earth are you doing?' more shocked than surprised.

He still held her in a vice-like grip.

'Let me go, Blake,' she said, wriggling out of his

144

grasp and standing in front of him, her eyes blazing. She was more scared than she realized.

'Oh, come on, Julie,' he said. 'Don't—'

'I beg your pardon!' Now she was furious, wanting to lash out but trying desperately to keep calm. Where had she read somewhere women who are raped frequently know their attacker?

'I think you had better go,' she said as coolly as she could, and made to brush past him to the door.

But with one hand he stayed her. 'No need to get so shirty,' he said. 'After all, what's good for the goose is good for the gander.'

'And what's that supposed to mean?' She imagined he was referring to Sybil. He put out a tentative hand towards her.

She felt her heart begin to beat fast. 'What do you mean?'

'I mean, my dear Julie, "when the cat's away,"' and walked back into the salon and sat down again on the sofa.

She followed him, furious.

'What do you think you are doing?' she asked. 'I asked you to leave.' Her heart was racing.

He took a deep breath, and gave a deprecating smile. 'Julie, dear, don't tell me you don't know what's going on?' He gave her a disbelieving look.

She stared at him. 'Going on?' Her mouth was dry. She had an awful feeling she was going to hear something she didn't want to hear.

'I thought you knew – sorry, Julie,' knowing that she wouldn't rest now until she did know. 'I thought you knew about the affair – Maurice's affair with Elaine Redmond.'

She couldn't believe what he had just said. 'Elaine Redmond?' The words came out as a whisper.

'Yes, my dear, Elaine Redmond, who lives at number

eighteen. She was an old girlfriend before you came on the scene.'

She sat down abruptly. 'You are disgusting,' she said. 'How dare you come in here telling me lies like this!'

He got to his feet. 'Well, suit yourself. No good will come of pulling the wool over your eyes,' he said pityingly, and got up and walked out of the room through the hall.

She followed him. 'I don't know what you are up to,' she said. 'Making trouble, though, I can see that.'

He glanced at his watch. 'Late back, isn't he?' He opened the door himself and walked down the steps. Turning he smiled at her.

'None so blind, Julie as those . . .'

She slammed the door after him. Oh, my God! It wasn't true, it couldn't be true. She felt physically sick.

She flopped on to the sofa, her heart beating wildly. She had dreamt the whole thing – it just couldn't be. But what was his point in telling her? Was it because she had rejected his advances? But that was a terrible thing to do if it wasn't true.

She went into the kitchen and poured a large glass of wine, taking it back with her, going over and over again his words. Affair . . . Elaine Redmond . . . why, everyone knew what Elaine Redmond was – a wealthy young woman with a very unsavoury reputation. Didn't she do some kind of voluntary work at the War Office? Julie shuddered. Downing the wine she went to the kitchen and poured another, bringing the bottle back with her – anything to stop her thinking clearly until Maurice arrived home.

Over and over again she recalled Blake's words. What had made him come this evening? Had he come specially to tell her? Was it because she had rebuffed him? What was more to the point was how could Maurice possibly . . . that woman . . . she wasn't his type at all . . .

146

She poured another glass of wine and slowly her eyelids drooped; oh, God, don't let it be true. She knew she was getting drunk, but that was better than ... and where was Maurice?

When she woke later it all returned. There was a horrible taste in her mouth; she rose unsteadily to her feet and staggered to the bathroom, took a shower and tried to pull herself together. She cleared away the glasses they had used and the small bowls. She hadn't dreamt it then, he had actually been there, sitting there, telling her that monstrous lie.

But where was Maurice? Had he had an accident – was he hurt?

By five o'clock in the morning she had convinced herself that Blake had been lying. For reasons of his own he wanted to set the cat among the pigeons. Yes, that's what it was. Had he seen Maurice with that woman, and jumped to conclusions? But what about Elaine Redmond? Had they met by chance, and with his sort of mind Blake had put two and two together ...?

The doubts crowding in again, filling her mind with torment, she saw it was beginning to get light outside. Rain was falling steadily, rivulets ran down the windows, and then came the first real crack of thunder.

And Maurice was not yet home ...

Lights were glimmering, a car started up, a taxi drove by and gradually the day began. Where was he now?

An ominous feeling of dread overcame her – why wasn't Maurice home?

A great flash of lightning lit up the room, and she gave a little cry – she hated storms. Was he safe? Had he been caught up in the storm? Glancing at the clock she saw it was seven-thirty. She poured herself a long glass of water.

She was at the window watching when she saw

Maurice's car – saw him get out and look briefly at the car, hurry to the door and open it. Now he was inside, his car keys thrown on to the hall table, his briefcase on the floor.

His face lit up at the sight of her. He took off his hat and she saw then the fair blood-streaked hair, saw the bandage on his wrist, the contusion on his forehead, all accusation, all bitterness, all the pain of suspicion was swept away as she threw herself into his arms.

'Oh, Maurice . . . Maurice! What happened?'

He held her tightly. 'Oh, nothing much, just a slight accident. I had to go to the hospital – the blood was pouring – hey, hey! Darling, I'm all right, I'm fine.'

And she knew then she would never refer to Blake's visit, never mention the name of Elaine Redmond, knew without the shadow of a doubt that she loved this man, that if he wanted another woman she must have failed him somehow, that in her heart she didn't believe Blake's story was true.

She had one more thing to do, though . . .

It was just as they finished breakfast, just before they set off for Walton Street.

'Darling, Maurice, could we dispense with Blake's services, do you think? We don't really need him now, and—'

He looked across the table at her, at the blue eyes which had looked serene and now looked troubled. Sometimes in the mornings she plaited her long thick hair and let it fall down her back. He loved that – it reminded him of his Dutch ancestry. Now the dark eyebrows accentuated her light eyes which looked so honestly back into his.

She never liked Blake Forrest, he thought. I wonder—

'Well, Julie, of course! He's ready to go. Did us a good turn, sure, but . . .'

That week their first child was conceived.

148

Chapter Twelve

James Maurice de Gruyt was born in 1946, a seven-pound boy with sandy-coloured hair and his father's fair skin and blue eyes, eyes that turned to brown as he grew older. Just like the dark eyes of his grandmother de Gruyt, who fortunately was still alive when he was born although she never saw him. He was just seven days old when she died; it was as if she was waiting for his birth before relinquishing all claim to this world and entering the next. Mrs Jones said she died with a smile on her face, so sure was she of the heavenly paradise awaiting her.

Both Julie and Maurice were delighted with the birth of their son, who helped to minimize Maurice's grief at the death of his mother. They had been very close always and he was overjoyed at the knowledge that his mother was alive when little James was born.

He thought he had never seen anything so beautiful as Julie and the expression on her face as she looked down at her newly born son. Her fair hair, thick and lustrous, curling into little tendrils where it was damp with her exertions, her cheeks flushed, her eyes darkened by wonderment as they met his. Julie was fascinated by this small scrap delivered into her arms by a midwife. She had had every attention at home, and Maurice insisted that she have a nurse, particularly as Julie wished to get back to work as soon as possible, which was something he wouldn't sanction.

'Not for some months, at least,' he said firmly and Julie knew it was no use arguing. So the nurse stayed on for eight weeks, followed by a nursemaid, though it was Julie who pushed his pram into the park for walks, enjoying every moment. Oh, wouldn't Gwen have loved to have seen him. She often thought about her.

When James was a month old Julie's parents came up from Wales to see him and stayed for a few days. They were delighted with their first grandchild and quite overcome with their daughter's lifestyle and surroundings, especially when she took them to see the small shop in Walton Street. How lucky she had been with her parents, she thought; they were such good people.

Between sightseeing, they talked about old times, and the war being over, and announced their intention of staying in Wales. 'We like it there, we've made lots of friends. We don't think we could return to South London now. All that bomb damage, it's so depressing.' Julie had never been back either. One day, she would – when she was ready. Only a few miles away, but it was another world.

'You'll never guess who came to see us the other day.' Nancy said.

Julie shook her head.

'Josef.'

'Josef who?' Julie was tucking the baby down into his pram.

'Eileen's friend.' She was able to talk about her daughter now without her eyes filling with tears. 'He is going to stay in this country, he says, somewhere near Slough – still in the Air Force.'

'Oh, that's nice.' Julie kissed her mother. Things were very warm now between them, now Julie had someone of her own to love.

Bob looked at them both, proud as a peacock. He could never get used to this tall elegant young woman who had achieved so much in her young life and had now given him his first grandson.

After they had gone, Maurice and Julie got down to dealing with his mother's death and the business involved. There was plenty to do, for Maurice was determined to sell the cottage which had belonged to his mother in Cornwall and buy something nearer to London – Kent, perhaps, or Sussex. Somewhere where they could go for weekends and holidays.

When Jamie was eight weeks old, and Nurse Cayley left, Maurice drove them down to Cornwall together with the young nursemaid. The house was locked up, but Mrs Jones had left the key. She had kept everything spotless and had gone to live with her son and his wife in a village near Truro.

Maurice saw to it that she was financially independent, for she had served his mother for many years back in Inverness Square as well as at the cottage.

They spent a week there, watching their baby in his folding pram, seeing the lovely colour in his cheeks from the country air. They took walks, and browsed around the antique shops in the local towns picking up something here and there which took their fancy. They were almost sorry to leave when the time came.

The day before they left, Maurice gave the keys to a local house agent, and arranged for the furniture to be removed to London.

'Aren't you sorry, darling?' Julie asked. 'Your mother was so happy here; it's a beautiful spot.'

151

'We have to move on,' Maurice said. He was never in doubt when he made a decision. 'Cornwall is impractical for weekends. We'll find somewhere nearer and enjoy it just as much.'

Julie was happy to leave the decision-making to him.

Once home they settled back into Inverness Square, the first thing they saw on their return being the SOLD board outside the Forrest's house. They had recently bought a place in Chelsea from where they would run their business. Although Maurice saw Blake now and again Julie never did, being careful to keep out of his way. They never socialised and once he had left the shop and Julie had became pregnant she made sure she never crossed swords with him.

She hardly, if ever, thought about that disastrous night. Having made her decision, she stuck to it. No good came of dwelling on such misery, and she had enough to do with her life without thinking about the whys and wherefores of Blake's tales . . .

Towards the end of the year, the lease of the shop adjoining their premises in Walton Street came on the market, and in the throes of negotiating the new lease in Church Street, Maurice decided to take the bull by the horns and sell it. He would amalgamate his gallery with the antique shop in Walton Street – it would be so much more practical – and Julie was pleased, knowing that they would be once more working together as a team.

One evening he came home to tell her he had spent the day with his solicitors; everything had been signed up and he had also bought the freehold of the house in Inverness Square which had become available and had put it in her name.

She gasped. 'Maurice! But why? Why not in our joint names?'

'It seemed a good business move, and this way you will always have the property to sell if anything happens to me.'

'What do you mean, if anything happens to you? Nothing is going to happen to you!'

'I am ten years older than you, and believe me, I know what I am doing. It's a safety measure; I took Roald's advice.'

Roald Mortimer was his solicitor. She frowned. 'Still, I wish you hadn't. It was your mother's house.'

'And now it is yours,' he smiled. 'Come on darling, anyone would think I'd thrown something at you!'

She smiled and went over and kissed him. 'Will I have to pay for the upkeep and all the repairs and that sort of thing?'

He rumpled her hair. ''Course not, you goose, we do have a joint account. See how much I've taught you about business, eh?'

When Jamie was a year old, Julie went back to part-time work in Walton Street and quickly got back into her stride, once she'd familiarised herself with the stock and prices, leaving Jamie at home with his nanny.

She began to attend the big auction sales which had started up again soon after the war, and enjoyed this part of the business more than somewhat, learning how to hold back, not to be carried away and learning that sometimes there would be losers as well as winners and not to be disappointed – it was all part of the game.

The two premises were opened up to become one large gallery after planning permission had been applied for and granted. The salon was stocked with wonderful paintings, some of which Maurice had got out of store where they had lain for several years. They needed to be cleaned and restored, all of which was a heavy expense, but the overseas buyers flocked to purchase while prices were still low enough after the war. Astute art dealers knew that in time prices would soar – they would be bound to – there were only so many Monets and Goyas and Rembrandts in the world.

When Jamie was four years old, Julie became pregnant again and that year her father died. It was a sad time – she took time off to go to Wales to be with her mother, who insisted on staying on in the village where she and Bob had been so happy.

'I've got good friends here,' she said. 'Don't worry about me, I'll be fine.'

As 1952 approached, on a dull December day Julie gave birth to a daughter, Olivia – a small, dark-haired girl weighing six pounds.

Both she and Maurice were overjoyed at the new arrival, while Jamie stood by the baby's cot looking down at her.

'She's not very big, is she?' he frowned. Julie thought he had probably expected someone big enough to play with.

'She'll grow, darling,' she assured him, 'and don't forget who's coming to see us tomorrow.'

'Granny!' he cried. He adored his grandmother Nancy, his only grandparent. She spoiled him and took him for walks in the park and Kensington Gardens to see the Round Pond and Peter Pan.

Maurice took on a new assistant, Petrie Havers, a young man with an art degree who specialized in Dutch painting. He proved to be a great asset and Maurice

154

thought he would keep him on when Julie returned to the business.

The House of de Gruyt prospered, as did most businesses that were any good after the war. Despite the heavy war loans to be repaid, the cost of the war being astronomical, Britain was slowly finding its feet and there was a renewed enthusiasm everywhere as efforts were made to pick up the pieces of the disastrous six years of conflict.

Julie had a new housekeeper, a Mrs Dobson, a war widow who was glad to find a home with a nice family. She kept an eye on the young nursemaid, and together with a cleaning lady who came once a week the house was well looked after.

Julie loved her life as a housewife and mother, but there were times when she ached to get back into the business, so deeply had she become involved in the world of antiques. Maurice was insistent that Olivia should be a year old before Julie could think of going back to the House of de Gruyt.

One day she pushed the high London pram through Hyde Park, Jamie being at nursery school. She was to collect him on her way home. She had become more and more aware of trees, seeing them through the babies' eyes, lying in their prams wide-eyed in wonder at the branches above them, the different kinds of trees, so majestic, looking as if they had been there for ever. She wished that they put the names on the bark so one would know what they were; at least she knew the names of the wonderful trees in Inverness Square, the towering plane trees, none of which had been destroyed in the bombing, as had so many London trees. She turned off to the path leading down to Kensington Gardens, in order to allow

Olivia to see the pond and the small boats sailing on it. She was sitting up now, her blue eyes dark with wonder as she looked all around her. There were only a few people in the park this morning, mostly walking dogs, or nursemaids pushing prams. Coming towards her was a tall well-built man who looked slightly familiar. Fairish hair, a well-cut sports jacket, he held himself with a certain air. Looking at him she saw that he was staring back at her. He came to a stop in front of her at the same moment as she did.

'Julie!'

'Les – Les Daly!'

She couldn't believe it, and impulsively he put his arms around her. 'Oh, it's so good to see you!' She was breathless – it was so unexpected, so unreal that he should be here after all this time.

Somewhat embarrassed, he released her, and she remembered that she hadn't seen him since the awful day of Gwen's funeral. Oh, but it was nice to see him, someone from the past—

He looked down into the pram. 'My word, what a beautiful little girl—' and Olivia looked up at him and smiled.

'Olivia, my daughter – she's ten months old.'

They both played for time.

'Well,' she said at length, 'What are you doing up here?'

'I live here,' he said. 'Well, not here, but in Kensington. I have a small house.'

'Oh. Let's push along to that seat. You must tell me all about yourself,' she said, and they walked slowly side by side. She sat down, putting the brake on the pram, while Olivia looked all around her. Julie couldn't think when she had been more pleased to see someone.

He was still handsome, and she wondered if he had married again – she had so many questions to ask him.

'Well, first of all, how are you? You look blooming, and no wonder with that lovely child.'

'Yes, and I have another, a son. He is five and at nursery school.'

'Of course, you live up here – in business, I recall. Antiques still?'

'Yes. We have a gallery, a salon in Walton Street.'

He was impressed. 'Oh, very nice.'

'Yes, it is. I usually work there, but I've taken time off for Olivia. I shall be going back soon.'

She turned and faced him, seeing the same face, yet older. He was a man now, not a boy, a young husband.

They had so much to talk about.

'Well, you haven't told me what you are doing up here—'

'Oh, sorry. Well, you know after the war my mother died, and I left the Navy and started in business on my own, wine shipping. It's the only thing I know.'

'Oh, wonderful!' Julie said, and she meant it.

'Yes, I've five shops – and I spend my time going back and forth to the Continent. It's quite a busy life. My main one is in Kensington so I made that my head-quarters, as it were.'

She longed to ask the question on her lips, but realized it was no business of hers. He answered it for her.

'I never married again,' he said. 'Never got over Gwen going like that, really.'

'I know. I miss her too,' she said.

'A couple of friendships, nothing serious. I suppose business keeps me busy.'

She thought of another seat in a park, she and Gwen, watching two boys playing tennis, the walk home – it

157

seemed light-years away. Who would have thought they would be together now on a seat in London's Hyde Park.

'I—' he began.

'You know—'

They laughed as they began to talk together, and Julie realized they were both slightly nervous instead of being at ease with each other.

'You know we were lucky to escape the war,' she said. 'So many friends died or were killed – my sister Eileen, Gwen . . .'

'Your sister – I'm sorry.'

'Yes, a bomb on Notting Hill Gate. It was awful – but so many people suffered.'

'My mother, too, died of her injuries subsequently – the landmine that fell on Balmoral Street.'

Julie had let out a gasp and covered her face for a moment.

'Didn't you know?'

'No, no, I had no idea. We lost touch moving away, Mum and Dad to Wales . . .'

Now they were relaxed and talking again like old friends. When Olivia began to get restless, Julie glanced at her watch.

'Goodness, it's twenty to twelve. I have to pick up Jamie,' and she stood up, reluctant to leave.

He got to his feet immediately. 'I'll walk along with you to Albion Gate,' he said turning to face her as she took the brake off the pram.

They walked in silence until they reached the gate.

'I'd like to see you again; is that possible, Julie?'

She looked into his eyes. Possible. Yes, but not probable . . .

'That would be nice,' she said.

Then the traffic stopped for her to cross and on the

other side she waved to him. He watched her go. Well, he told himself, it wasn't likely. She was probably happily married, he hadn't asked her that, but judging by the look of her she was, with that lovely baby and a son.

He walked back through the park to Kensington: perhaps he would see her again. The ridiculous thing was it was Julie who had attracted him in the first place, with that air about her – she still had it. Gwen, bless her, was so warm and chatty and pretty, and he had loved her. Yes, admit it, he had loved her. When she was killed he was devastated and had never tried to replace her.

Julie now was a different kettle of fish. The way she walked, the way she looked at you – he could remember all those years ago – those blue eyes, the tears, then could only remember the funeral and dear, dear Gwen.

Seeing Julie had brought it all back, that wretched time in his life, and now he took himself in hand.

What's past is past, he told himself as he had done so many times. Time to get on with the future – no use crying over spilt milk – and he walked briskly towards Kensington.

Julie could not get over meeting Les Daly – what a shock, but a pleasurable shock. He hadn't changed that much, older, of course, and wondered if he thought she had . . .

'Look, darling,' she said as they approached the house on the corner that served as a nursery school, and tipped the pram so that Olivia could see Jamie when he came out with his striped blazer and school satchel.

She squealed when she saw him, waving her arms up and down.

Jamie handed Julie a drawing.

'For me? Oh, that's lovely!' she cried and he looked so chuffed. She refrained from asking 'What is it?' for it wasn't too clear.

159

She bent and kissed him. 'Thank you, darling, Daddy will be pleased.'

With Jamie's hand on the pram, she walked on home.

Only later, after dinner, when the children were in bed, did she remember her meeting with Les Daly.

'I met an old friend today, in the park,' she said.

Maurice turned a page.

'Did you darling? Who was that?'

'A friend from my schooldays.' To her horror, she was blushing.

Maurice looked up. 'That was nice . . . How was she?'

'It was a he,' Julie said.

'Ah,' Maurice said knowingly. 'An ex-boyfriend.'

'No. Gwen's husband.'

'Oh, I'm sorry, darling, your friend who died.'

'Yes.'

'How was he? In the Navy, wasn't he?'

Fancy Maurice remembering that. 'Yes, he has a chain of wine shops now.'

'Crowded market,' Maurice said. 'I wish him luck.'

Maurice never minced his words.

Chapter Thirteen

In the Walton Street showroom, Julie came out of the
stockroom carrying a velvet tray on which sat a set of four
silver coasters dated London 1794. They were beautiful;
the silver gleamed where they had been polished, and she
placed them carefully on a blue velvet shelf in the window.
They would not remain there long, she thought.

Standing behind the glass cabinet, she eyed the
contents: Georgian and Victorian jewellery, antique
watches; jewellery was not her particular forte. She
loved the furniture best of all, particularly the smaller
pieces, so hard to find. As soon as they acquired a small
piece, it invariably sold quickly.

Her eye fell on a small Chinese enamel ewer, just over
six inches high, painted in famille rose colours with
European figures. Eighteenth century – how she would
love it. But they were busy building up the business, and it
would take time. Almost all Maurice's capital had gone to
fund the gallery and the purchase of the freehold of
Inverness Square. But the war had been over for almost
ten years. Jamie was at his prep school and Olivia at the
nursery school, and she watched now as Petrie Havers
dealt with the sale of a small Picasso drawing. She loved to
watch him at work, and learned from him. Like Maurice

161

he was an expert on oil paintings, especially Dutch ones.

Back in the office, she glanced at her watch, and saw that it was almost time to pick up Olivia. She liked to do this every day, but if she wasn't there, Mrs Dobson would do it. She straightened Maurice's desk and flicked through the mail which came for him; he always had a lot of mail, much of it from Europe and overseas. One day, they promised themselves, they would take a trip to Europe and look up Maurice's relations in Holland and Germany and Switzerland. She looked forward to that, for she had never been abroad.

It certainly was not very likely this year; they had nothing planned, although she felt that Maurice needed a break. He had not looked well of late, but blamed it on the strain of building up a business in a new area. Sometimes she wondered if he missed the gallery in Church Street; he had been so much at home there – but he assured her he did not.

Today he had gone up to Tircross Manor, where Lord Tircross was proposing to sell some of his valuable art collection. Owners of large houses found the upkeep difficult and frequently had to resort to selling some of their possessions in order to help.

Olivia was waiting on the steps holding the hand of a junior teacher, and her eyes lit up as she caught sight of her mother. She looked down then up at the teacher.

'Yes, I know,' smiled Miss Dymchurch. 'Your mummy is coming,' and Julie, quickening her step, saw Olivia's dimple – just one – and her blue eyes, just like her own smiling back at her, her dark curls escaping from beneath her grey school beret.

'Hello, darling. Is that for me?'

Olivia held out a brightly coloured silver-papered egg – it was coming up to Easter.

'Oh, that's lovely, darling. Did you make it?' It really

162

was quite clever, she thought. You had to make the most of these lovely moments. They went all too quickly – no little drawings and eggs now from Jamie.

'It's not chocolate,' Olivia said, excusing the egg. 'But there is a surprise inside, and you mustn't open it until Easter Sunday, Miss Dymchurch said.'

'Oh, I shall look forward to that.' Taking Olivia's hand, she made for home.

Mrs Dobson had tea waiting for them; home-made scones, milk for Olivia and tea for herself and Julie. Julie always insisted that Mrs Dobson should sit down to tea with them, unless of course she had visitors, which was not very often. She lived a businesswoman's life – no social life for her. Sometimes she thought how different her life was from her mother's back in Balmoral Street where, at teatime, there was always a home-made cake, but the similarity ended there. The familiar smell of scorched cloth from the nearby range, the smallness of the kitchen, the washing either drying on a wet day, or ironed and put up to air on the overhead airer in the scullery, the duckpond bath standing on edge outside the kitchen window, the chickens scrabbling about, the brown eggs from the black hen . . .

'We break up tomorrow,' Olivia said.

'Yes, and Jamie too.' She saw Olivia's eyes shine at the prospect. She adored her brother. You would never have thought they were brother and sister, Jamie with his sandy-gold hair and dark eyes and Olivia with dark hair and blue eyes. During the Easter holidays she was going to take them to see her mother in Wales. Nancy Halliday kept fairly well, but she was ageing fast and missed her husband. The children simply loved the trip because they went by train.

While Mrs Dobson cleared away the tea things and the children had retired to their playroom, Julie laid the table in the dining room for their evening meal. Mrs Dobson always prepared the meal and did the vegetables so there was little to do. Maurice insisted on carrying on just as his mother had, although sometimes she thought it would have been easier to eat in the large kitchen. But she never argued with Maurice unless she really felt herself in the right. Then she could be stubborn.

She was surprised to hear Maurice's key in the door and glanced up at the clock. Almost five-fifteen – he was early. Sometimes he stayed at the gallery quite late, particularly if he had been out of town all day.

She went forward to greet him, kissing him, and noticing his pallor. 'Maurice, is everything all right?'

He sighed. 'Yes, darling, just another harrowing day.'

He was under strain, she knew. And there was nothing worse for getting a man down. He put his briefcase down and held her for a moment, and she could feel his heart pounding beneath his shirt. She frowned, sensing something was amiss.

'You would tell me if there was anything wrong, wouldn't you, Maurice?'

He smiled, but it was a weak smile. 'Wrong? Why would anything be wrong? Don't you worry yourself.'

He took out the mail from his briefcase, and Julie saw that it had been opened. So he had been back to Walton Street. He took the letters and went into the study.

'I'll just pop up and have a shower; I had a filthy journey.'

'Yes, all right, darling, and I'll have a drink ready when you come down.'

It was after the children had gone to bed and they were having coffee that he asked her when the children broke up from school.

'Both of them tomorrow. Why?'

'Well, I was wondering, why don't you go off at the

164

weekend and spend a few days with your mother?'

'You mean, on my own?'

'Well, Julie, I honestly don't think I can make it this time.'

'But it's Easter next weekend!'

'I know, but you go with the children. She'll love to see you, and to be honest I have a lot to do. We can't both leave the shop.'

'But it will close for Easter and Petrie will be there on Saturday.' She saw the look on his face that she had only seen there a few times, a look which meant he was not to be argued with, and she shrugged. 'Oh, well, if that's what you want. I thought it would do you good to get away for a few days. We could stay in that nice hotel and leave the children with Mother.'

His shoulders slackened. 'Yes, I daresay,' and he sighed. 'I am a bit anxious at the moment – but it's nothing really. You go off and give yourself and the children a break; you need one as much as I do.'

'It won't be the same without you,' she said, coming over and putting her arms round him where he sat with his back to her.

'Bless you,' he said. 'I'll make it up to you.'

So early one morning, she and the children took the train to Wales. There was great excitement at Paddington watching the steam trains arrive and depart, and when they finally boarded theirs they could hardly contain themselves, specially when they knew they were to have lunch on the train. They changed trains once again at Swansea for a local one and took a taxi to Granny's village which lay overlooking the beach, while in the distance they could see the cockling sands and the strange-coloured flames and smoke from the steel works at Llanelli where her father had worked temporarily during the war.

Nancy made a great fuss of them, couldn't believe how much they had grown since she had seen them for she no longer came up to London. The cottage seemed so small, tiny almost, but there were three bedrooms, and Nancy now slept in the one downstairs to save her walking up and down the steep, narrow staircase. The children would share one room while Julie would have the other.

Julie was reminded of Balmoral Street, but she would have to find the right time to tell her mother about the landmine and the horrific damage it had done – that's if she ever did.

Everything smelled sweet and fresh, the sheets, the air, the garden. It really was a breath of fresh air after London.

'We'll have some tea, then you can tell me all your news. I did wonder if you might come by car.'

'No,' Julie said, 'it's a long drive, and besides, the children just love going on the train and they don't get much opportunity.'

'They are beautiful children, Julie,' Nancy said. 'Jamie is so handsome, just like Maurice, and little Olivia is just like you, except for the colour of her hair.'

'She has your dark hair, Mum, it grows just like yours. See how it curls at the back.' Nancy looked as though she would burst with pride.

'I'm cooking a Welsh leg of lamb for dinner,' she said. 'Do they have an evening meal? I wasn't sure.'

'Yes, Jamie eats with us at home, but Olivia won't; she won't want much after this tea. She's dead tired anyway, although she won't give in.'

'You must be too,' Nancy said. 'I can't wait to hear all your news, but tomorrow is another day as they say. Let's clear away – and children, you might like to go into the garden.'

Granny's garden was magical; water coming out of a little stone boy Bob had made after the war, daffodils and spring bulbs grew everywhere, while early tulips were set in wooden tubs. The garden was small but being on a hillside the views were beautiful.

'I can't think how you manage to get up and down that hill to the village,' Julie said. It quite worried her.

'Well, I don't run up and down it,' Nancy said reasonably. 'And I don't do it every day. I manage. I miss your father though. But I have wonderful neighbours.'

'I'm really glad,' Julie said, trying to imagine what it might have been like had they stayed in Balmoral Street. 'I thought I might hire a car or taxi – is there such a thing here? and take us for some drives.'

'Yes, we're not exactly at the back of beyond,' smiled Nancy. 'We have newspapers too, and the Mothers' Union, and the church, and—' she added proudly, 'I have even bought a bottle of wine – Spanish. Oh, yes, I know what's going on in the world outside.'

Julie laughed – it was just like old times.

Nancy had gone grey, but she still kept her old hairstyle. She put an apron on to cook the dinner, much as she had in the old days. Her face was lined now, and her dark eyes had sunk deeper. She was after all, nearly sixty. Looked at like that she was doing quite well.

Julie met the neighbours, and they shopped in the village. They hired a car to take them to see the sand dunes and Nancy explained to Jamie how the Normans had taken over all those hundreds of years ago, had their own Lordship and castle, now in ruins.

'I'm very ignorant about Wales,' Julie admitted ruefully.

'Most people are,' Nancy said drily. 'But I can tell you it is a place full of interest. Of course I can't get about much now, but occasionally our Women's Institute goes on a trip and I love that. And of course, I read a lot. It really is very interesting, the history of Wales.'

Her mother never ceased to surprise her. In the evenings she heard all about the gallery in Walton Street. She had thought Church Street in Kensington was swish, but when Julie described Walton Street and its shops, she was very impressed.

'Josef – you remember – has gone back to Poland,' she said. 'He came to see me before he went – wasn't that kind? Such a nice man.'

Julie felt suddenly near to tears. 'Yes, he was—'

'I'm glad Eileen had him for a friend,' Nancy said.

Shall I tell her he was more than that – that they lived together? No! Julie decided. I've kept it to myself for so long. Let it rest.

'Yes, so am I,' she said. 'Eileen was very good to me when I started work in London,' she said suddenly.

'Was she?' Nancy looked so pleased. She stared into space. 'She was a very clever girl, our Eileen.'

'Yes, she was,' Julie said simply.

'Now children, bedtime,' she called, getting up and busying herself. 'We have to go home tomorrow.'

'Oh, no!' they wailed.

'What about poor Daddy. Don't you think he is missing us? All on his own?'

But this did not elicit a wave of sympathy, so she made a face at Nancy and began to clear away . . .

Olivia fell asleep in the train on the way home, and Julie gently removed her thumb from her mouth, and smoothed the curls back from her forehead. She would probably sleep all the way home, but Jamie was busy looking out of the window.

168

It was a long journey, and she got a taxi at Paddington to take them home, looking forward to seeing Maurice again after a few days away. They were so seldom apart – it probably did them both good to have a break.

He was at home, busy working in his study, but it was easy to see that he was preoccupied, although he was delighted to see them back home.

'I've missed you,' he said, holding her close.

'We've all missed you,' she said. 'It wasn't the same without you.'

'And we bought you a present and tulips from Granny's garden,' Jamie said.

The children were tucked up in bed, and they had partaken of Mrs Dobson's prepared meal of cold meat and salad, followed by gooseberry fool and coffee, when Maurice pushed his plate away, refusing cheese which was a favourite with him. She noticed then his high colour, his bright eyes, as blue as speedwell flowers, and realized that he was taut as a violin string.

'How has it been going at the gallery, anything interesting?' she asked casually, knowing he would only tell her in his own good time.

He put down his coffee cup and looked straight at her. 'How brave are you?' he asked quietly, and her heart plummeted like a stone.

Her lips felt stiff and dry. 'Brave?' she whispered. 'What is it, Maurice?'

'I'm in trouble,' he said. 'Big trouble.'

She felt slightly sick. 'Are you ill, darling? What's wrong?'

'No, I'm fine,' he said.

'Then nothing else matters,' she said staunchly.

'I wish I could agree with you.' He stared in front of him. 'To come to the point – they are doubting the

169

provenance of a Rembrandt we – I – sold way back in 1953.'

'Who is doubting?' she asked.

'The purchaser. Ultimately lawyers will be called in, and, I suppose, the police.'

'Oh, Maurice! How awful! Is it that serious?' she asked.

'Darling, when an expert sells a painting by someone like Rembrandt, he has to know what he is doing.' He sounded a little impatient.

'You must tell me about it, I don't understand. Did you sell it from Walton Street?'

'Yes.'

'What was it? Would I remember it?'

'I doubt it; a small painting, of a child's head, about ten inches square. Absolutely wonderful,' and his eyes held the reverence they reserved for art that was beyond price.

'So, who bought it?'

'An American dealer from New York – wanted it for a special client.'

'Presumably he paid a lot for it.'

'That's neither here nor there.'

'And you were able to give him the provenance on it.'

'Of course, or he wouldn't have bought it – had it scrutinized by Max Offert, vetted by the National Gallery, all that.'

'So what's the problem?'

'He is not doubting its authenticity, but where it came from.'

'And where did it come from?'

He hesitated. 'I said I bought it together with other works of art from, well, you know, your old employer – what was his name—'

170

'Not . . . not John Leeds!'

'Yes. It was on the list of paintings – one that my father sold his father, oh, way, way back.'

'And you bought it back when he sold up and went down to Devon?'

'Yes, that's it.'

She thought for a moment. 'I had to list everything, didn't I? Of course, I don't recall his having a Rembrandt, but then I wouldn't, not being well up in the art world.' She saw to her astonishment that his face had flamed a fiery red.

She hated to see him like this, at a loss – he was always so sure of himself. She put out a tentative hand and touched his. 'Maurice, are you telling me everything?' she asked gently. 'It hadn't belonged to the Leeds family, had it?'

'You may as well know the worst then you will be prepared,' he said wearily. 'No, I didn't get it from him.'

She was still. 'You mean, you lied.'

He made no answer.

'Where, then?' she said at length.

'I can't tell you,' he said. 'I'm sorry, I can't tell you.'

'But we shouldn't have secrets from each other, especially business secrets. Maurice, where did you get it from?'

'I can't tell you,' he said. 'I can't tell you.'

'You didn't steal it, did you?'

'No, of course not, I'm not a thief!'

'Then . . .'

'Oh, you wouldn't understand. You are so young, and I was such a fool – I never thought anything would ...' He buried his face in his hands.

But for once Julie stood her ground. That he had done

171

something wrong or unlawful was obvious, and she had to know it all. She couldn't possibly help him unless she understood.

Her lovely world seemed to have crashed all around her, and from such an unexpected source. 'Maurice, I can't help you unless I know the full story,' she said.

'No one can help me,' he said. 'I'm on my own – and I am just deeply sorry to implicate you.'

'But I am your wife.'

He sat staring in front of him, but all she could think was that he had lied. He had lied . . .

Chapter Fourteen

The next few days were a nightmare. They were extremely busy in the shop before it closed for Easter, although Petrie would be there on Easter Saturday, but nothing Julie could say would elicit further details from Maurice.

'Here is the letter,' he said, holding it out to her. It was from a lawyer in New York saying that his client, a Mr Moses Harris, had purchased a painting by Rembrandt from Mr Maurice de Gruyt in November 1953, and was now doubting the provenance given to him.

He and his client were coming to London in May and he would be obliged if Mr de Gruyt would make himself available for an interview. He remained, etc. etc.

Julie read it, her heart beating fast. This letter looked like business. No wonder Maurice was worried.

'And have you suggested an appointment?'

He frowned. 'Of course, my dear.' He sounded impatient. 'You don't ignore a letter like that – it's more than my life is worth.'

'Oh, Maurice, can't you tell me more about where it came from? Please, I will try to understand.'

'There are others who are implicated and I have no

wish to involve them more than I have to,' he said.

'Oh Maurice! You don't meant it is all part of a big—' swindle, she was going to say but thought better of it – 'operation?'

He looked at her, his eyes troubled. 'Julie—'

'Well, if you won't let me help,' she turned away.

'I don't want you involved,' he said. 'It had nothing to do with you.'

'But I am involved,' she said coldly, 'and if you won't tell me . . .'

'I suppose I am hoping it will all go away,' he said.

'But if something is wrong – illegal – it will come out eventually,' she said. 'I'm not so young and silly that I don't know that . . . I'm not a child any more, Maurice.'

'No, you are having to grow up too fast,' he said bitterly.

She dreaded May coming. He had not told her the exact date when the appointment had been made for fear of worrying her, she supposed and she felt more and more cut off from him. She had her days cut out working part time in Walton Street and with the children being home for the Easter holidays. Once they had gone back, she was determined to try and find out more about the mystery.

Her mind went back to the war years, when Maurice was away so much, at first abroad, he had told her since, and in later years at Bletchley Park. She knew he spoke Dutch, French and German which is why the government had wished to use him. Heaven knew what places he had visited. That part of his life was still a mystery to her. What upset her was the fact that he had lied about the provenance – why had he done that unless he had obtained it illegally? He had said he hadn't stolen it, and she was sure he hadn't, but he had lied, and it was more than an expert art dealer's reputation was worth to be found out in a lie. Why had he lied? Why not say where he got it – them – from if he had bought them legally? Round and round her thoughts went. The mystery deepened with no help from Maurice.

One morning she made up her mind. The memory of that evening with Blake Forrest came back to her for no rhyme or reason. The so-called affair Maurice was having with Elaine Redmond – what had that all been about? Why had Blake told her that? If Maurice was capable of lying over a stolen painting, would he deceive her in other ways?

Curiosity got the better of her. On the Friday morning, a morning she often took off for shopping, she took a taxi to Chelsea and made her way to Blake's small shop.

It was quite a come-down from the premises they had had before. Amidst all the bric-à-brac she could see Blake Forrest, still a good-looking man, but his hair was thinning and he had lost a lot of weight. She hesitated before going in.

What had she come for? She was in two minds to retrace her steps. Impulsively however, she pushed the door open, and Blake, recognizing her, came forward.

'Why, Julie – Julie de Gruyt! How are you; welcome to my new premises.'

She looked around and smiled. 'Plenty of stock, Blake.'

'Oh, yes, no shortage there,' he said. 'And to what do I owe this pleasure? Are you seeking something special, famille vert, the odd, as yet undiscovered Impressionist painting . . .'

She smiled. 'How are you both? It's ages since we've seen you and Sybil?'

He looked straight at her. 'Sybil's left me – didn't you

know?' he added as he saw her shocked face.

'No, I didn't,' Julie said. 'I'm sorry, Blake.'

'Yes, so am I,' he said. 'Still, there we are . . . luck of the draw. You and Maurice still together, I hope.'

She smiled again, picking up a small Mason jug and looking underneath.

He had given her an opening. 'We might not have been if I had believed your ridiculous story that night you called in at Inverness Square.'

She put the jug down and saw him go a fiery red. 'You certainly didn't believe me,' he laughed.

'I certainly didn't.' They were both playing for time.

'I've often wondered, though,' she said idly, still fingering the jug, 'why you came up with such a ridiculous story?' And he laughed out loud.

'I fancied you,' he said.

'Oh, is that all?' she said. She was damned now if she was going to ask him if there was any truth in it. She was sorry she had come.

'Mind you,' he confided, 'it wasn't totally unfounded. I'd seen them dining together once or twice.'

'They were old friends, before I came on the scene.' Julie said.

'No, I mean after – still, if a bloke can't dine with an ex-girlfriend . . .'

She was convinced he knew no more than that, and she wasn't going to probe further – she felt too sick inside. What was the truth of that story?

'I'll have that little jug,' she said, delving into her purse.

'Not quite your thing, is it?' he asked, wrapping it.

'I collect little jugs,' she said, and thought: now *I'm* lying.

'Thanks, Blake,' she said. 'Well, good luck, see you

176

sometime,' and left the shop, her heart beating nineteen to the dozen.

Dining with her, was he? Elaine Redmond . . . Whatever happened to her?

Sick with herself that she had sunk so low as to try to fathom out Blake Forrest's story all that time ago, she hurriedly caught a taxi to Kensington High Street. Paying the driver, she wandered into the shops, browsing but not concentrating, furious with Maurice for not confiding in her, for holding secrets from her. It was his fault. He must think her a child. She couldn't imagine her parents having secrets from each other – but then the circumstances were different. This was something on a grand scale. Did Maurice think she was too young or not intelligent enough to be told the truth . . .?

She walked through the cosmetics department in Derry and Toms, clutching her little jug. She would have it out with him that evening. Things had gone on long enough.

She walked along Knightsbridge until she came to the park entrance, breathing deeply to quiet the turmoil going on inside her. She sat on a seat presently, watching the passers-by, the girls in the fashion of the moment, tight waists and full skirts, hair tied back or in curls. But she wasn't really seeing anything until a man stopped in front of her, and she looked up.

'Les Daly!' She was genuinely pleased to see him.

'Julie, my dear – may I?'

'Of course,' she said as he sat down beside her.

'This seems to be a favourite meeting place,' he smiled. 'How long ago was it – must be three or four years . . .'

'Well, Olivia is almost five now, and she was in her pram.'

'How are you?' he said, noting that she didn't look at

all well. Not blooming as she had been all that time ago. She was pale, the blue eyes troubled and there were little frown lines between them.

'I'm fine,' she lied. 'How are you?'

'Very well – business is good – I still have my headquarters in Kensington, hence my walks in the park.'

She was surprised at how pleased she was to see him. Someone from the past – a link – an untroubled time when they were young. He looked so familiar.

'I've been to Knightsbridge,' she explained, 'taking advantage of a morning off.'

'Children at school, I suppose?'

'Yes, I often take Friday morning off, shopping, that sort of thing,' and hoped he wasn't thinking she was giving him an excuse to see her.

'Well,' she amended 'any morning really when we aren't busy.'

'It's a full life, isn't it? Running a business and bringing up children. My mother found it so – not that she ever complained.'

Julie smiled. 'She was quite a character, wasn't she?'

'She was indeed. I missed her when she died.'

He was so comfortable to be with, perhaps because he was English, Julie thought. Maurice was English – born here – but of Dutch parentage. Did that account for the lack of understanding between them?

He had an urge to take her hand in his and it wouldn't have been the first time in his life. But he would be taking advantage – he could see how tense she was. It wasn't his business though – she was a married woman, and as far as he knew happily married.

'How is your husband? Maurice, is it?'

'Yes, he's fine,' she said staunchly. So that wasn't the reason. 'How is the business going? Wine, wasn't it?'

178

'Growing fast. I've four more shops now – can't keep pace since the war with the wine trade; used to be mainly Spanish and French of course, now they're going for Italian. I think we're becoming a nation of wine drinkers.'

'And aren't you pleased it's not beer then?' she smiled.

'Oh, that too,' he laughed.

'What about Gwen's parents?' she asked. 'Are they still alive?'

'The old man is. Her mother died. Never got over the shock of Gwen's death.'

'I can imagine.'

Several pigeons settled around them, pecking at the dry ground.

She was still, still as a statue sitting there, and he felt she didn't want to get up and make her way home.

'I nearly got married again last year,' he said suddenly, as much to get her out of her apathy as anything.

'Oh, Les, that's wonderful! You say nearly – what happened?'

'I got cold feet – it's as simple as that. I think it becomes more difficult the longer you are on your own. It's been some years now, and I wasn't looking to replace Gwen so much as find a wife I could be happy with, have children.'

'And so you should!' Julie said. 'You must get awfully lonely living on your own.'

'The business is time-consuming, and I travel a lot.'

'Still, it must be awful coming back to an empty house.'

'I have a housekeeper,' he said.

'Oh.'

179

'An elderly lady,' he said. 'Like my mother.' He smiled at her.

She glanced at her watch. 'Goodness, it's eleven forty five – I must get back.'

She stood up, drew on her gloves and picked up her handbag. Then she held out her hand.

'It's been nice seeing you again, Les,' she said.

He wanted to lean forward and kiss her for old times' sake – but knew that he wouldn't. He didn't want to embarrass her further.

'Hope to see you again, Julie.'

'Yes, you must . . .' but the words died away. In view of what awaited her at home, she couldn't possibly invite him to dinner. Besides, no good would come of that.

'I go this way,' she said.

He watched her out of sight, her high heels clacking on the path, her back straight with that upright walk of hers, then turned and walked on towards Kensington.

Julie hadn't wanted to leave him. He was nice, stable, a link with the past where everything until the war had been like that. Now, everything was changed; what was she doing up here in the centre of London in a prestigious antique business with a husband who would not be open and honest with her? Perhaps they had too little in common; perhaps he would have been happier with the Elaine Redmonds of this world. And why did Gwen have to die, leaving Les alone? She thought of Balmoral Street and their neighbours. Life was so much quieter then when the biggest problem was what she and Gwen were going to do when they left school . . . but it was no good going down that road – it was another world with Eileen alive. No, she must get on with the problems of today.

'You've made your bed,' her mother would say, and she was right. You made a decision and you had to stick to it, whatever happened. She had loved Maurice, had wanted to marry him. Was she going to desert him now that he was in trouble? Imagine what he must be feeling – after all, his whole reputation was at stake; he had so much to lose. She hurried along faster, anxious to get home and change. A quick lunch, then back to Walton Street, to take her place in the gallery while Maurice was at an auction at Sotheby's.

She thought it out carefully. She would present him with an ultimatum. If he couldn't, or would not tell her the real story behind the provenance of the Rembrandt, she would leave home and take the children with her. Go to her mother's. But she couldn't possibly stay with this hanging over her head without knowing the real truth behind it all. She would do it this evening, once the children were in bed. She felt better now that she had made up her mind.

They ate their meal in constrained silence, Maurice preoccupied, Julie getting more and more nervous at what she was about to do. The children provided a pleasant diversion – and what about them? she thought. They were involved in this too. Their father perhaps about to face serious charges. Oh, what was the end of it all to be . . .

'Have you finished your homework?' she asked Jamie.

'Yes. I did it before dinner,' Jamie said. He was due to go to boarding school soon, the same school that Maurice had been to.

'Will you come up and read me a story?' Olivia asked.

'Yes, off you go, say goodnight to Daddy.'

Maurice bent down to kiss her, ruffling her dark curls. 'Sleep tight.'

It was towards nine o'clock when Julie finally came downstairs having tucked them both up in bed and sorted out their clothes ready for the morning.

She found Maurice downstairs, a glass in his hand, standing by the window overlooking the square.

'Join me?' he asked.

'Yes, please,' Julie said, seating herself in an easy chair.

He brought over a glass and handed it to her.

'Thank you,' she said and there was something in her tone that should have told him this was not going to be an evening like any other.

'Maurice; I have something to say to you.'

'Yes, darling.'

'Maurice, I want you to tell me the story behind the real provenance of the Rembrandt.'

He stared at her. 'You are not serious?'

'Yes, I'm afraid I am, Maurice. If you are not going to trust me, I shall leave you and take the children with me.'

He covered his face with his hands; it was as much as she could do not to go over and comfort him.

Presently he took his hands away and sank into a chair. 'Just give me time to think,' he said.

She was very calm. 'I have all night,' she said equably.

Chapter Fifteen

When Maurice finally spoke, the words were dragged from him.

'The Rembrandt was obtained illegally . . .'

Julie was stunned and felt a little sick, still unable to believe it. That Maurice would do such a thing . . .

She finally found her voice. 'You had better tell me everything if I am to understand.'

'Yes, of course,' he said flatly. 'In 1940,' he said, as if the date was imprinted for ever on his mind, 'April of that year, I was in Holland – but you wouldn't have known. In fact you know very little about my activies during that part of the war. Of course everything was of the closest secrecy. All of us knew that—'

'Us?'

'Oh, there were many of us, all doing our bit. There are things that have never come out about that war in Europe – particularly in Switzerland. Today the mind boggles at what went on.'

She realized that this was going to take some time, but he was better left to tell it in his own way.

'You know there was a great deal of money – and of course valuable works of art and jewellery – owned by many wealthy people and corporations in Holland and

Belgium, and the owners fell over themselves to find places of safety for it until after the war. That is unless they could get it overseas, to England or America, but that was not always possible. That is why the Swiss banks did so well; millions and millions were stashed away in Swiss banks, some of it never to be found again, I daresay.' His lip curled. 'But I am talking about art. Our government and our banks – the Bank of England particularly – were fed information about money and stocks and shares and so on being removed from banks in Belgium and Holland and France. As the Germans moved deeper into these countries and each town or city fell, ownership of properties and banks came into their hands, so information was passed to London about just how much money or particularly stocks and bonds and their numbers – all the relevant information was passed to the Bank of England and the War Office. The City was working overtime in more ways than one. But I was only concerned with art . . .'

He paused, then went on.

'There were a great number of Dutch people, many of them Jewish, who owned wonderful paintings, and of course they were under constant threat of death. Many of them would disappear without trace, and many more went in fear of their lives. It was a terrible time; I can hardly bear to re-live it. You cannot imagine some of the atrocities that went on.' He sighed deeply. 'One elderly Jewish family owned the painting we are now talking about, the Rembrandt – I had seen it before – the most wonderful painting I think I have ever seen.'

He had quite forgotten she was there, but went on, 'I knew, because he – the owner, Abraham Lewitz – had told me sometime previously that he was going to hide it. He didn't trust banks, and, with several other pictures and drawings, he found what he thought was a safe place and

184

paid an old servant to look after them ... Shortly afterwards he was taken away by the Nazis together with his whole family.' His hands were clenched, the knuckles showing white ...

'I will spare you all the awful details – they would only upset you – and get to the important part. I don't suppose you remember Elaine Redmond? She used to live in Inverness Square ...'

Julie's heart missed a beat, and she felt the colour rush to her cheeks. 'Wasn't she an ex-girlfriend of yours?' she asked trying to keep her voice steady.

He frowned. 'An ex-girlfriend? What are you talking about, Julie?'

'I thought—'

'I don't know where you got that from. I went to school with her – nursery school. There used to be one in Inverness Square – her nanny was a friend of my nanny's and used to take us to the park together. We went there until we were seven.'

This other world, thought Julie. But he did dine with her.

'Well, Elaine worked at the Bank of England during the war temporarily – she had quite a brain – and so of course she was one of those given inside information as to what was going on. She had to take down the particulars from the banks and finance houses and galleries which came over the telex minute by minute as each town and village fell. She telephoned me one day and asked me to meet her for lunch, said she had something to tell me – she knew I was on secret service ... we'd always kept in touch.'

Lunching? wondered Julie.

'Well, over lunch she told me that she had heard that several important pictures had been hidden and she knew their whereabouts – knowing me and my background and my love of Dutch art and going over to Holland quite a bit she thought I might be interested.'

'And you were,' Julie put in, knowing what was coming next.

'Yes, I have to say, I was, particularly in the Rembrandt.'

'I am not going to tell you exactly how I managed it, nor the exultation I felt, and still do at getting hold of it right under the German noses. It was the greatest feeling I had ever experienced. It was small, I brought it back with me in my special holdall – and well, that was that.'

Julie frowned. 'You haven't told me all of it. How did you get it, where was it, who actually gave it to you . . .'

'The old retainer – of course he knew me by sight – had seen me before, and knew that probably his days were numbered. I could have had many more paintings, but of course, I wasn't interested – only in the Rembrandt.'

'Of course,' murmured Julie, and she frowned. 'I mean, what did you give him – anything?'

'Of course I did. I gave him a thousand pounds in Dutch money. It was a kind of exchange so that at least he had something of value and I signed that I had received it. It was not the value of the picture at the time – it had no value in those terrible times . . . As far as I was concerned, making sure the Germans didn't get hold of it was some kind of recompense for him; his employers had gone; he was a broken man, but at least he had some money to buy food. I didn't steal it, Julie.'

'No, but you weren't entitled to it, either,' she said.

'You mean it would have been better to let events take their course, and let it end up in some fat German's household? I couldn't, I just couldn't.' He buried his face in his hands.

186

'Well, to sum up, you paid for it – almost bought it, at least, but still you acquired it illegally.'

He looked up. 'Yes, I did.'

'Then what?'

'I sold it in 1953 – the figure escapes me, but I can look it up – to an American, this Moses Harris from New York, and I gave the provenance, as, well, you know, as coming from John Leeds. I said I had bought it back from him, his father having bought it from my father in 1920.'

'Which was a lie,' she said. 'Oh, Maurice!'

'Yes, that's the worst part,' he said. 'Lying about the provenance.'

'Couldn't you have said you bought it from someone in Holland during the war? Or before the war?'

'I couldn't have backed it up. I would have needed something in writing, a deposition, and I never thought there would be repercussions. After all, Harris was satisfied it was a genuine Rembrandt. It's not that that we are fussing about.'

'It's hardly fussing, is it?' Julie said. She was still shocked to the core that her Maurice could do such a thing. 'I'm thinking of you and your reputation.'

There was a long silence.

'The meeting is arranged for 11 May,' Maurice said at length. 'I don't know what they have in mind . . .'

'Is it an indictable offence?'

'You mean, can I be arrested? I don't know. I shall know better after the meeting. My solicitor, Roald, is a bit worried. He says to his knowledge it's the first time this sort of thing has cropped up, although he thinks there will be many occasions in the future when it does.'

'Well, we are only concerned with what happens to you. Oh, Maurice.'

'I am disgusted with myself for putting you in this

position,' he said miserably.

'You took an awful chance,' she said, 'and now you are having to pay for it. I wonder why Mr Harris queried it. What did he know or suspect?'

'We won't know that until the meeting's over; it's being held in Roald's chambers.'

Getting through those few days was a kind of hell. There was nothing either of them could do but await the outcome of the visit of the American, Moses Harris, and his lawyer, and Maurice's lawyer, Roald Mortimer. The morning Maurice set off for his appointment saw both of them in a high state of anxiety.

'Well, it's not the end of the world,' Julie said as she kissed him goodbye and wished him luck. 'We're in this together – what's to be will be,' giving voice to an optimism she was far from feeling. 'I'll be waiting for you back at the gallery. Mrs Dobson is going to see to everything. I've told her we won't be back until later.'

How she got through the day Julie never knew. She was on her own, having sent Petrie to an art sale in Petworth; he would not be back until the next day.

It was almost five o'clock when Maurice arrived back at the gallery and a quick look at his face told her the worst.

She ran forward to greet him, putting her arms around him, seeing the expression on his face, and thought at that moment she loved him more than she had ever done. How must he be feeling?

He flopped into a chair. 'Well, they're not doubting its authenticity,' he said. 'So that's something, but it's the only good thing.'

'I'll get you a drink,' she said, and locked the door of

the gallery and pulled down the door blind.

He wasted no time in getting down to details knowing how anxious she was. 'To put it in a nutshell, it seems there are still members of the Lewitz family alive. There were grandchildren, but they all disappeared and this is a cousin, Anna Lewitz. Long-lost, but authenticated – who is now demanding the return of the Rembrandt to her family—'

'Oh, Maurice! Who is she?'

'The daughter of Abraham Lewitz's brother, who miraculously escaped the fate of the rest of the family. She is elderly, but of course, within her rights.'

'Maurice, when you did – this – did you never think that in the future something like this might happen?' She had a sudden thought. 'Maurice, is this the reason that you put Inverness Square in my name? In the event that there might be—'

'Well, I wasn't thinking of that particularly, but it did occur to me that in this business you forget sometimes how liable you are for mistakes or wrong judgement; so much depends on your word. The damages can be high . . . Roald advised me and I took his advice.

'My only thought,' he went on, 'was to get it out of the country. My mistake was selling it and of course not being able to provide the correct provenance.'

'So you supplied a false one,' Julie said, and saw the frown on his face. 'We have to face up to the worst of it, Maurice, otherwise we can't deal with it. What does he intend to do, this man Harris? And how did he find out?'

'Firstly he wrote to the Leeds . . .'

'Oh, no!'

'He had to. He learned that Mrs Leeds had died but John Leeds was still alive, and denied ever having owned the Rembrandt – which, of course, he would.'

Julie's cheeks were hot. She hated the idea that John Leeds had discovered what Maurice had been up to; he would be ashamed, as she was. Strange that he had never got in touch with them, never telephoned. She guessed it was to save them further embarrassment.

'Then, of course he made inquiries – that's what has taken so long. He went back years to the time before the war when the Rembrandt was in Abraham Lewitz's possession, followed it through, put two and two together—' He put his head in his hands. 'God, what a mess!'

'What do they want you to do now?' Julie asked. 'What's the next step?'

'To put it in a nutshell, they want the Rembrandt to be returned to the Lewitz family, and the House of de Gruyt to recompense Moses Harris to the tune of, well, whatever the Rembrandt is worth today.'

'What do you think that is?' Julie found she was whispering, she was so fearful of the answer.

'It is practically priceless, I can't imagine what it would fetch at auction. I shall have to get expert advice, of course, but that is all they will settle for.'

'Isn't that a kind of blackmail?'

'Yes and no. Harris is honest enough to want to return the painting to its original owners, but why should he lose over it? He bought something in genuine faith which is not legally his and he wants recompense for that.'

'But we couldn't, could we?' Julie said. 'It would be a fortune. Will they settle for what it would fetch on the market today?'

'They'll have to.'

'We have the house.'

'No, that's yours.' Julie thought how astute he had been. Had he suspected something like this might happen?

'You must have it back; we must get the money somehow – sell the business—'

'But even that might not be enough. I'll be bankrupted.'

It was nine o'clock before they reached home, exhausted with talking, his solicitor's words ringing in Maurice's ears: bankruptcy, the business to go, he would lose everything. But there was a long way to go yet, so much to work out.

Everything was forgotten when two days later Julie's mother had a heart attack.

'I must go to her,' she said. 'I'm sorry to leave you at a time like this, Maurice, but Mrs Dobson will take care of everything. I don't know how long I shall be, but I have to go.'

'Of course you do, Julie, and you mustn't worry about anything back here. I'll cope with any problems.'

Oh, why does everything have to happen at once, she thought, sitting in the train speeding on its way to Wales, still seeing Maurice's anxious face as he waved her goodbye at Paddington. For the first time in many weeks the main worry on her mind that of her mother.

She bought a bouquet of flowers at the station and hoped they would last out the journey. Please God make it work out all right.

She made her way to the cottage hospital where her mother had been for the last two days, and was directed to the women's ward.

Her mother lay with her eyes closed, her greying hair loose around her shoulders. Julie so seldom saw her with her hair down that she hardly recognized her, she looked so young and vulnerable. She tiptoed to the bedside. At least there were no screens around her, so perhaps she was not in danger. She put the flowers on a side table, and stood there silently. Presently Nancy's eyes opened and when she saw Julie standing there her eyes filled with tears and she put out a hand towards her 'Julie—'

With a lump in her throat Julie bent and kissed her.

'You're going to be all right,' she said. 'I'm here now and I am going to stay until you get better.'

Nancy gave a wan smile.

'Oh, you are a good girl to come all this way and leave the children. Lovely flowers, thank you.'

'The children are fine, Mum, and send their love – Mrs Dobson and Maurice are looking after them. I can stay as long as you like.'

She imagined her mother walking up and down that steep hill, getting out of breath, and felt guilty that she hadn't put pressure on her to move away to a more suitable area; but her mother had loved her little house and probably wouldn't have listened, and so she comforted herself, guilty nevertheless that she hadn't done enough. What was a business and all its problems when you were faced with a crisis like this.

'Were you alone – when—'

'Yes, it was towards morning.' Nancy's voice was low and indistinct.

Julie took her hand. 'Never mind, I'm here now—'

'Mrs Nelson was very good. I tapped on the wall and she heard me. She called the ambulance.'

Thank God for good neighbours, Julie thought. She would have a word with the ward sister when she left, or the doctor, if that was possible.

The ward sister was at hand to answer any questions, but she was not very hopeful about Nancy's condition.

'She has had a heart condition for some time, did you know?'

'No, she never said.' Julie answered.

192

Typical, the ward sister thought. The children were often the last to know.

'Well,' she said kindly, 'it was quite a severe attack and caught her unawares, but she is in good hands and we are doing all we can. Will you be staying in the area?'

'Oh, yes, at her house, and I shall be in again to-morrow, any time I can come?'

'Well, your mother is on open order,' the sister said.

'What does that mean?'

'She can have visitors at any time.'

'It's serious, isn't it?' Julie asked.

'Well, she is not a young woman, but a lot depends on her will to get better. She must rest, that's the main thing.'

'I'll see she does,' Julie said, hoping that Nancy's will was strong enough together with her heart to pull her round, that she wasn't still fretting too much about Bob going and leaving her alone.

Nancy lived for two more days, suffering another major heart attack in the small hours.

Julie was distraught, overcome with grief – it had all happened so suddenly. She made her way back to the little house, sitting by Bob's pond and stone boy, and wept and wept until she could weep no more. Only then did she telephone Maurice and tell him the sad news.

'I'll be with you as soon as I've cleared up here and told Mrs Dobson, don't do anything until I arrive. Have a stiff drink, you need it, and try to rest.'

She had never been more pleased to see anything than Maurice's car coming to a standstill outside the house.

He took her in his arms. 'Julie, darling.'

Chapter Sixteen

There was not a lot of clearing up to do in Nancy's house. She had kept it spotless and it was a rented property, so the keys were just handed back to the landlord. After taking a few personal mementoes for herself, Julie offered anything she might like to Mrs Nelson who had been so good to her mother. Several neighbours were pleased with pieces of furniture and when Julie left with the few things she had wanted, she turned her back for the last time on that little terraced house on a hill in Wales, the home where her parents had been so happy.

Maurice glanced at her – he knew what she was going through, and knew too that she was going home to even more problems. But he saw the set of her chin. Tragedies, he thought, strengthen us, and he hoped that it would be so for Julie . . . He needed her as he had never needed anyone in his life before.

Once home she explained gently to the children what had happened, and saw their serious little faces, Olivia trying hard not to cry. They had loved their grandmother.

It was not until the next day that Maurice got down to brass tacks, knowing she was anxious about the outcome of his talk with his solicitor.

'We are going to need an awful lot of money, Julie,' he said, 'capital that I ploughed into the acquisition of the premises in Walton Street, the stock, the purchase of the freehold of Inverness Square . . .'

'Yes, I've been thinking about that,' she said.

'I have been inquiring of all the big auction houses and art dealers about the possible value of the Rembrandt.' He hesitated.

'Yes?' she pushed. 'You can tell me, I'm past being shocked.'

'Well, they came up with a figure. At today's estimation . . .' He mentioned a sum that made her blink, but that was all as he waited for her to say something.

'And you will have to find that money to clear yourself with Mr Harris?' she asked.

'That's what everyone agrees is the thing, the only thing to do.'

'And the picture is restored to its rightful owner this—'

'Anna Lewitz—'

'Are all the lawyers agreed on that?'

'Yes, all I have to do is find the money. And Julie—'

'Then we shall find it,' she said. 'I don't intend to let this get us down. We shall find a way, and I have been thinking.'

How, Maurice wondered, had he been fortunate enough to find this fair-haired English girl who had been so young when they married, with no real experience of business, and who was prepared to stand by him? He didn't deserve her.

For a moment Julie thought he was going to break down. 'Firstly,' she said, 'we must make sure that the children don't suffer. I suggest we go along with Jamie's new boarding school as planned. Yes, I know the fees are high – and then Inverness Square.'

'Well, that is yours. I was going to—'

'We shall sell it,' she said. 'We can get quite a high price for it, and it will bring whatever the painting is worth – I hope. I shall go to see the agent and get an idea of its value.'

'But—'

'You said it was mine, Maurice,' she said gently. 'You handed it over to me, presumably to do as I liked with. Well, it is the most important thing we possess and we need the money – if it is not enough we must sell everything else we can, but keep the House of de Gruyt going as long as possible for Jamie's sake. Already he seems to take after you, and if there is one thing they can't take away from you, Maurice, it is your inherent knowledge of paintings. You could even,' she smiled, 'work for one of the big people, Sotheby's, Christie's, as a fine art consultant, or whatever they are called. It is not your expertise which is in doubt, is it?'

When he said nothing, she went on.

'Have we Mr Harris's word and the solicitor's that not a breath of this will reach anyone outside except the only people concerned?'

'Absolutely. They will sign to that effect.'

'Then we have nothing to fear.' She reached out and took his hand.

'Julie, I feel so guilt-ridden. You cannot imagine my feelings. To have to give up Inverness Square – my father bought it – and look how I have let everyone down.'

'No time for self-pity,' Julie interrupted brusquely. 'Let this be the last time I hear you talk like that. We have to get down to business – quite literally – and sell some of the furniture in Inverness Square. Yes, I know it belonged to your mother and is valuable and so on, but

196

we may need it to sell to make up the money.'

He looked up at her, and she could have wept at his expression; defeat, failure, everything a man dreads most Maurice had had to face up to.

'You haven't said where we shall live,' he said, as if the answer lay with her, and her only.

'I thought we would rent a flat,' she said, pressing on, 'in a cheaper area; Bayswater, Kensington . . .'

'Oh Julie!'

'What's wrong with that?' she said with a cheerfulness she was far from feeling. 'It is only a temporary measure until we get on our feet again. Jamie will be at boarding school so there will be just the three of us. We'll manage.'

The flat in Pulsbrook Street, Bayswater, was on the first floor with a large sitting room-cum-dining room, a kitchen, three bedrooms and a bathroom. They had access to the garden from a balcony with iron stairs. Maurice looked around with disfavour, but Julie laughed.

'Yes, I know it's not what you're used to,' she said. 'But you should have seen Balmoral Street. Look, the ceilings are nicely plastered with Victorian frescos, the doors are nice. It has been quite a prestigious property, Maurice.'

They moved in, with a bedroom for each of the children, and a somewhat antiquated kitchen – but then, so had the kitchen been in Inverness Square, except that it had been enormous with massive cupboards and lots of room.

Jamie started his new school in September and Maurice insisted that Olivia continue with her nursery school. They settled down into their new lives. By December the sale of Inverness Square was under way, and in the New Year all the legalities had been overcome, the deal signed, and the Rembrandt on its way to its new owner. Once it arrived, Mr Harris sent Maurice a copy of a letter sent to him showing Anna Lewitz's gratitude.

'My one regret is losing Inverness Square,' Maurice said.

'But there was no alternative; we couldn't have raised enough money otherwise, and you never know,' Julie said with her usual optimism, 'one day it may come back on the market. Maybe by then Jamie will be able to buy it.'

The whole affair had taken a year out of their lives, and as time went on, Julie realized that it had been even more of a blow to Maurice's self-esteem than she had appreciated. He had lost so much of his self-confidence – was only half the man he had been. Such a blow had knocked him sideways, and having to live with himself and the knowledge of what he had done to Julie and his family sometimes seemed more than he could bear.

He hated the flat in Pulsbrook Street and took to going for long walks in the park rather than stay inside it. The House of de Gruyt prospered. All his attention now was given to the business, and he worked hard travelling all over the country in the hope of finding a treasure. He was called upon more and more by the big auction houses; prospective purchasers were all given his name for reference.

Petrie Havers was still with them, and now business was picking up more than ever. After the long war years people were spending money on their homes and wanted only the best, investing in antiques. They found it more and more difficult to find time to go to sales and pick up fine pieces which necessitated going to more auction sales and buying privately. With this in mind, Maurice took on another assistant, William Castle, a middle-aged ex-army officer who had previously worked for Blane's, the big art dealers, and Julie took on a young girl straight from finishing school, Lady Suzy Grimm, an earl's daughter, whose father had decided she had better do something with herself rather than fritter away the time before settling down and marrying good money. Heaven knew they needed it – the family was broke.

Suzy, at nineteen, with wonderful hair and legs that seemed to go on for ever together with her laid-back attitude, was an asset to the business. The de Gruyts gave good value when training staff, putting the not inconsiderable sum paid to them by Suzy's father for her training to good use, while Suzy's decorative value was a bonus. Not that her heart was in it, but as she said it was a stop-gap until she decided what she really wanted to do. Not her fault, Julie thought, that she was born the daughter of an earl. In another time and another place she could probably have been a successful young woman in her own right, but there was precious little incentive to change her lifestyle.

Julie glanced up at the clock and decided it was time to close. Maurice had gone down to Somerset for a house auction where there were reputed to be wonderful Turners for sale, and would not be back until late that evening.

She decided to close the shop and called Suzy who was outside having a quick ciggie, and was even now spraying everywhere just in case old Julie found out, unaware that the fumes followed her wherever she went.

'Time to close, Suzy,' she called.

She would be pleased. She could never wait to get home to what she called her partying which to Julie seemed to go on endlessly any time she was not working.

Suzy sauntered in, swaying like a model, to lock up and close the front door, while Julie went back into the office where she found William and Petrie poring over the books.

'How is it going?' she asked them knowing that the auditors were due next week, but she and Maurice had no fears about that; William was an excellent bookkeeper, and the two men got on very well although they were so different.

'I've asked Suzy to lock up,' Julie said. 'Don't work too late.'

'Goodnight, Mrs de Gruyt.'

'Goodnight.'

She turned the key in the door to let herself out, and almost bumped into a man who had been looking in the window.

He stood up straight, touched his cap, and smiled with pleasure.

'Julie!'

'Les!' she was genuinely pleased to see him.

She looked older, he thought, but still the same Julie – tall, willowy, her thick fair hair pulled back, blue eyes smiling up at him.

'Can I help you?' she asked like any shopkeeper.

He grinned. 'I was window-shopping,' he said, 'I often pass this way. You have some lovely things here, Julie.'

'Thank you. Well any time do call in . . .'

'Are you off home?' he asked.

'Yes, I am.'

'In a hurry?' he asked. 'Do you feel like joining me for a drink – or coffee?'

'Well . . .' She hesitated. Maurice would not be home

200

until late, and Mrs Dobson was with Olivia. What harm would there be in that?

'Yes, I'd like to.'

He was probably quite lonely, she thought, as she fell into step beside him. Poor Les. How long was it since she had seen him? Over a year, surely.

'In here suit you?' he asked outside a prestigious hotel.

'Yes, this is fine,' she said, as he held her arm and led the way to the cocktail bar and lounge.

'Are you sure? We can go into the other room where it is quieter if you like . . .'

'No, this is fine,' Julie assured him.

'And what will you have?' He saw her hesitate. 'Will you join me in a dry Martini?'

'That would be nice,' Julie said, never having had one. She and Maurice only ever drank wine and Maurice the occasional whisky.

He ordered from the waiter, while Julie removed her gloves and eased off her jacket. It did seem odd to be drinking with another man.

'Well, tell me how you are – and your delightful children. The boy must be . . .'

'Growing fast,' she said. 'Away at school. I think he will eventually follow his father into the business.'

'Ah, that's always nice,' Les said, 'at least for the father.'

As the waiter brought the drinks, he stole a look at her. She was still lovely, but at a guess, she had been having a bad time. There were signs of strain around her eyes, the blue eyes were not as wide and innocent as they had been, but then, like him, she was older and life wasn't always easy in business. He was dying to ask her if she was happy, but he didn't want to pry. What did he really know about her? That he had always been a little in love with her even when he married Gwen? And seeing her that time in the park had disturbed him more than somewhat.

As they sipped their drinks, Julie realized she had not been so content for a long time. He was easy to be with, Les Daly, a comfortable man she would have said, not the sort of man to bring trouble to a marriage; he would protect his wife. She reproached herself immediately for the uncharitable thought. How could she compare Les Daly with Maurice? They were worlds apart . . .

'I suppose you wouldn't consider following this with dinner?'

'Oh, well, I really should—'

'Oh, please, do, Julie, for old times' sake.'

'Well, I suppose I could . . . Maurice won't be back until later. He's gone to a house sale.'

So he was still in the picture, Les thought. Well, he should have known, but he would enjoy talking to her over a meal.

Why not, she thought suddenly; it's time I had a break from business.

'Yes, I'd like that, Les,' she said.

'Good, I'll book a table,' he called the waiter over.

Dinner was an impromptu affair, but none the less enjoyable for all that. They talked over old times, Balmoral Street and the neighbours, who they could remember and she told him how her mother had recently died. The time simply flew past until she realized that he hadn't really told her anything about himself.

She saw him for what he was, a handsome, successful man, well dressed, with those kind eyes that were never one colour – bluey-green, tawny it was one of his attractions – eyes that really looked at you, and his golden skin colouring at odds with that fair, sleek hair.

'And you, Les?' she asked. 'What about you? Are you happy?' He put his hand over hers on the table, and she felt the warmth and a curious kind of elation, then withdrew her hand slowly from under his, just for a moment imagining what it might be like to give in to desire and fling her bonnet over the windmill. It would be so easy with someone like Les.

'I might have guessed, you're still in love with that husband of yours,' he said to cover up what was a big disappointment. He had always secretly believed that something might come of his knowing Julie Halliwell, but had never understood how it would come about. Still, she had a special place in his heart.

She adopted a playful manner. 'Don't tell me there is no one special in your life, Les!' She smiled across the table at him.

'Oh,' he laughed. 'They come and they go. As a matter of fact, I did recently meet someone. I still see her, although I'm not sure about marriage. She wants it, but ...'

She stifled a swift pang of jealousy. 'You should have children, Les; you would make a good father.'

'I like to think so.'

'And nice to have them while you are still young enough to enjoy them,' she said seriously. 'What is she like, Les?'

'About my age, works in the City, lives in Kensington. As unlike Gwen as it is possible to be.' He nearly added: but a lot like you ...

'She sounds nice,' Julie said. 'Les, what are you waiting for?'

You, I suppose, had been on the tip of his tongue, but he didn't say it.

'You are not getting cold feet are you? No one more

unlikely to be a confirmed bachelor than you, Les.'

They faced each other across the table and their eyes locked, knowing what was in each other's mind. Julie was the first to look away. Yes, she thought, it could have been wonderful, and Les thought, he doesn't appreciate her, this . . . Dutchman, whatever he is, but it's too late now, I see that.

'Well, this has been lovely, Les,' she said, finishing her coffee and crumpling her napkin.

'Lovely to see you, too,' Les said. He knew now that he must accept the situation. It was never going to be otherwise. He was chasing rainbows. She would be his dead wife's best friend, a girl he knew when they were both young; for ever.

'Well, thank you for the meal, Les,' she said, drawing on her gloves.

'We must do it again some time,' he said, knowing they never would.

He called a taxi for her, and held her hand for a moment, not kissing her.

'Bye, Les. And thanks again.'

In the taxi she sat back, her head resting against the cushion. Her life was like two separate worlds. One belonging to Balmoral Street, her childhood, Gwen and Les Daly – then the real one, as the wife of Maurice de Gruyt, the great art dealer, part owner of the House of de Gruyt; mother of two children.

It was then that she understood that she had never really been in love with Maurice, not in the way she loved Les Daly. She admired Maurice, liked him, was impressed by him and all that he stood for, but that special spark had been missing. One touch from Les Daly was all it needed to bring it alive. Was this what most women settled for in marriage, or did they marry their Les Dalys? She and Les might have married, been unhappy, fought even, but the passion was there, for want of a better word . . .

Dear Maurice, the father of her children. How could she even be thinking this way? Just because she had dined with the man who was a link with her childhood, he hadn't even been a boyfriend. It was Gwen who had married him . . . if Gwen hadn't died she might never have seen him again . . .

The taxi stopped, and she got out and ran up the steps to the flat where Maurice was waiting for her.

'Julie,' he kissed her, 'I was worried. You didn't leave a message.'

'Sorry darling,' she said, 'I met an old friend, and since you weren't coming home until later . . . Have you eaten?' She peeled off her gloves.

'Yes. I stopped off in Bath on the way back and had a meal.'

'Just let me change and I'll be with you, then you can tell me about your day. Did you find anything nice?'

It was back to business.

Chapter Seventeen

And then the Sixties came in with a boom.

The Beatles, Biba, Mary Quant and mini-skirts – young people seemed to take over the world, not least among them Jamie de Gruyt, who had opted for art training. London became the centre of the universe and tourists flocked in their thousands to Carnaby Street and the King's Road where every possible fashion flair could be seen. It was as if everyone was carried along on a wave of euphoria. Older people said the roaring Twenties had never been like this. Music played from every possible outlet, and with the boom came business.

In the middle Sixties, Jamie took his place on the staff of the House of de Gruyt and Olivia at fourteen was more sophisticated than Julie had been at twenty.

Business was spiralling. There were now six staff in Walton Street. To ease pressure on living space, Jamie got himself a flat which he shared with two other young men, both in the same line of business.

Julie and Maurice knew they must move soon – they were so busy in the gallery they found little time for anything but finding stock and selling it – but kept putting off the day.

Lady Suzy had long gone. She had married well, much

to the delight of her father, and often came in to spend some of her husband's fortune, made in the post-war boom selling prestigious cars – Bentleys in particular, especially old ones. Derek, her husband, thought her adorable and while he was not of the top drawer, nevertheless, these things seemed to matter less and less in this day and age. Besides, as a result the old family home was able to restore the roof and a few more rooms and put in some bathrooms. Derek had insisted on it.

In her place came Elizabeth, better known as Tizzy – a ravishing girl of nineteen anxious to pick up all she could about the business. She had a particular affection for silver, and had done a silver course, still keeping up her classes, so eager was she to learn.

Maurice thought her excellent material, and an asset to the business, but he was not quite prepared for Jamie to fall for her hook line and sinker.

Julie saw it another way, 'Don't be hard on them, Maurice, they are mad about each other.'

'Yes, but far too young,' Maurice said. He promptly dispatched Jamie off to Paris to do six months with a famous art dealer. He enjoyed it so much he stayed a year and perfected his French. In the meantime, Tizzy had left to go to Christie's where they thought much of her.

Jamie came back, almost twenty-two, and settled down again in the House of de Gruyt.

Olivia had a great interest in interior decor, but it was not surprising considering her background, Julie thought. She was given a course at Mrs Maxwell's prestigious premises in Knightsbridge.

It was the busiest time of their lives when, out of the blue, in 1971 Maurice had his first heart attack.

Shocked, because they had had no warning, life was

suddenly turned upside down. After a spell in hospital, a nurse was installed in the flat in Jamie's old room until he got better, but it was some months before he returned to Walton Street.

Julie watched him like a hawk – he seemed so frail – and the following year they went for their first proper holiday, a cruise to Madeira. It seemed to do Maurice the world of good and he returned to London much fitter. He had put on weight, and his outlook was much more hopeful, but sometimes Julie felt that he had never been the same since that awful business about the Rembrandt. Something had happened to him then, something he never really got over. But she rarely thought about it now; it was past and gone. Even Blake Forrest was gone. He had moved himself down to Brighton, a much more suitable place for him, Julie thought, not a little bitterly.

The Seventies had come in with flared trousers, huge collars and men with lots of long hair, sideburns and tight-fitting shirts. By now it was an accepted fact that you would wear what you liked, no one cared – decorum had gone out of the window.

One weekend, Jamie suggested he should take them out to dinner, which was such an unusual thing that Julie and Maurice decided he must have something to tell them. They knew he had been going out with a girl for some time, but he had never brought her home.

'I've a surprise for you,' he said. 'No, don't try and worm it out of me, Olivia – it won't work.'

The table booked, they waited in the foyer for Jamie to arrive, and when he did it was with Tizzy, a smiling, radiant Tizzy on his arm.

'I don't believe it,' Julie gasped. 'Where have you been hiding her?'

'We wanted it to be a secret until we were sure – and now we are. Tizzy and I are engaged.'

'Oh, darling, that's wonderful!' Julie exclaimed and kissed Tizzy.

'I sent you to Paris to forget this young lady,' Maurice said, but he looked pleased.

'It didn't really work, Dad,' Jamie grinned. 'Tizzy used to come over to Paris for the odd weekend.'

Julie was shocked, no one seemed to mind what they said these days.

'Are you happy about us, Julie?' Tizzy asked. 'I love him dearly.'

And that's another thing, Julie thought – Julie. In the old days I would have been Mrs de Gruyt. Nevertheless she turned smiling eyes to Olivia.

'My dear, we are delighted.'

'And another cog to the wheel, Dad,' Jamie said.

'Clever boy,' Maurice said, patting his arm.

They were married the following year at St Paul's in Knightsbridge, Tizzy a radiant bride in a traditional white gown carrying pale pink roses and stephanotis with Olivia as her only bridesmaid. The reception was held at Searcy's, hosted by Tizzy's parents who lived in Holland Park.

Tizzy was absorbed into the House of de Gruyt as if she had never been away.

Two years later, she gave birth to a son, whom she called Maurice. Her father-in-law was thrilled. She came back to business after six months, leaving the baby in the charge of a Norland nanny with whom she knew he would be safe.

It was at Olivia's suggestion that the firm expanded to take in interior decor.

'The one thing goes with the other,' she said. 'When you do up a house, you need lovely things to put in it. Why not start up another business: House of de Gruyt: Interior Decor?'

What an ambitious young lady she was, thought Julie. But she was right – to be successful you had to expand and Maurice was very keen on the idea.

'It'll take some thinking about,' he said. 'Not something to take on lightly.'

He and Julie were in the process of trying to find a house; after all these years they had grown out of the flat, although Olivia had moved out to live with another girl in Notting Hill Gate.

A sad look had passed over Julie's face when Olivia told her, remembering her own sister who had lived there, and who had died in the bombing raid.

'Whereabouts in Notting Hill Gate?'

'Just off Church Street,' Olivia said. 'Chartwell Mansions.'

Well, it would have been rebuilt by now, Julie thought, trying not to re-live it all again. It had been the saddest time of her life.

They had found what they thought would be a suitable house in Kensington when Maurice had his second heart attack, so all thoughts of moving were abandoned. He was in hospital for some weeks, and came home a shadow of his former self. He was worried about the business and insisted Julie should return, assuring her he would be quite all right and needed only to rest and be reassured that all was going well at the gallery.

The children came in to see him all the time; there was nothing he liked more than hearing news of the gallery.

'Sold the Gauguin today, Dad.'

Maurice's eyes lit up. 'The *Pont Aven?*'

'Yes. It'll leave a blank on that wall, though.'

Maurice knew the feeling. 'Still, well done!'

The doctor insisted that only rest would do Maurice good; relaxation, rest, good food and no worries.

Well, Julie thought, business has never been so thriving – we have no problem there. A super son and daughter-in-law, a simply beautiful grandson, and the knowledge that Tizzy was pregnant again pleased her more than somewhat.

Elizabeth Juliet was born five months later and, a month later, Maurice died. Without any warning. He had been reasonably well, but Julie woke up one morning with a kind of premonition. Looking across at the next bed, she saw that Maurice hadn't moved from the night before. The bedclothes were still in the same position, his head half buried in the pillow, and she jumped up and ran to him. He was cold – how long he had been dead she had no idea. She telephoned for the doctor immediately and he came at once.

He stood up after examining the body. 'I should think he has been dead some hours,' he said. 'Died in his sleep, which is a great comfort, Mrs de Gruyt, although it must be a shock for you.'

The children came and wept – they had loved their father – and Tizzy was a tower of strength. How sad life would be without him.

He was buried in Kensington churchyard near his father, and Julie returned to the business knowing that now she would more than ever rely on the children for help.

One late afternoon in May, just as they were closing the gallery the door was opened and in came a tall man accompanied by a woman. He was well dressed, looked affluent, while the woman with him was attractive, fair, and, Julie guessed, some ten years younger than him.

Les, Julie thought, it's Les Daly.

'Good afternoon,' she smiled at him, going forward. 'How nice to see you again.'

He had put on some weight, his face was plumper, but she would have known him anywhere.

He smiled at the woman beside him.

'I'd like to introduce my wife to you,' he said. 'Pat, this is Julie, an old friend of mine.'

'How do you do?' Pat said. 'I've heard so much about you.'

I wonder what he told her, Julie thought, before replying, 'So nice to meet you,' and taking the outstretched hand.

'Well ...' Les turned and smiled at his wife. 'We are here to buy an anniversary present – our fifth wedding anniversary.'

Julie assumed her business expression. 'Congratulations,' she said. 'Did you have something in mind?'

'Pat has her eye on that Georgian ring in the window, the one with the yellow stone.'

'Then allow me to take it out for you.' Julie went over to the window and asked the young assistant to unlock the door for her.

Lying on its velvet bed the ring, with its large stone flanked by small diamonds, winked up at her and she held it out to Pat for her to try on. Julie's expert eye saw the platinum wedding ring, the other two diamond rings and the single signet ring on the little finger of Pat's right hand. She was a lady who lacked nothing in material things, obviously. Then she took in the soft kid gloves carelessly placed on the glass counter and the exquisitely long painted nails. She had a very attractive face, well made up, and was dressed beautifully. I think, Julie decided, he is happy with her. I'm glad for him.

While fittings were taken for the ring, which had to be made smaller, Les turned to Julie and smiled. 'We have a baby son, eighteen months old,' he said proudly. A shaft of pure jealousy tore through Julie to be quickly replaced with joy at the news.

'Oh, how wonderful!' she cried, 'you must be delighted,' and she saw the way he looked at his wife.

'And how are you Julie?' he asked. 'Is your husband well?'

Her eyes fell. 'He died some months ago.'

She looked up and for a brief moment their eyes met. Then everything fell back into place.

'But I have two beautiful grandchildren,' she went on.

'That's wonderful,' Les said. He turned to his wife. 'Well, darling, what do you think?'

'It's beautiful, Lesley,' she said, and leaned forward to kiss his cheek as Julie busied herself with details of the sizing and whether the ring would be sent or called for.

It would be called for, Les said, and they took their departure. Julie watched them go, her blue eyes inscrutable.

A few months after Maurice's death, she saw an advertisement in *The Times* for their old house in Inverness Square, and, her heart thumping loudly, knew what she had to do. She must buy it back, however much it cost – for Maurice's sake . . .

She summoned Jamie and the rest of the family and a joint decision was made.

Number Twenty-Five Inverness Square must belong to the de Gruyts again and there would be no one more pleased than Maurice if he knew . . .

Six months later she was installed in the house where

she had started out with Maurice during the war years. It seemed very strange to be back, but once she had their own furniture and pictures up it began to look like home.

The house was big enough for all the family; Jamie and Tizzy had the large bedroom, and the children the top floor, while Julie had the second bedroom, and the big kitchen more than housed them all. Olivia opted to stay in her flat. Once given her freedom she was not going to relinquish it easily.

One evening Julie sat in the drawing room overlooking the square, browsing through the art catalogues of forthcoming sales, when Lot No. 23 caught her eye.

Lot 23. Oil painting by REMBRANDT, UNKNOWN BOY. 10 × 10 ins. (Property of Mme Anna Lewitz (dcd.))

She sat staring in front of her, the tears pouring down her face . . .

Chapter Eighteen

2000

Inside the house in Inverness Square all was still. Sue Greenwood was alone in the kitchen, her feet up on a stool as she read through the daily paper, glad to sit down for a spell. Soon she would serve tea to the children and grand-children. The cake had been made, Mrs de Gruyt's favourite lemon cake and Sue's famous scones were ready to be warmed and buttered and spread with home-made jam and cream. There was a time when she worked round the square for various families; everyone wanted Sue's help, she was good-natured, reliable and honest, a lot to be said for these days – but now she worked almost full time for Mrs de Gruyt. If one of the family wasn't there she would stay overnight; you couldn't leave the old lady alone, not that she would have complained, she was as tough as old boots.

She was resting now upstairs in her room and Sue glanced up at the clock. Three forty-five; there would be no need to wake her, she seldom slept in the afternoon. Rested was what she called it ...

Julie de Gruyt, as she was known to everyone in the square, was the oldest resident, not in years, but in occu-pancy. Arriving there as a bride in the Second World

War, she had deemed herself fortunate to live at such an elegant address as Inverness Square, which she had done except for a few years after the war.

She herself was a Londoner and people might think she had been exceedingly lucky – fallen on her feet as the saying goes. Well, she supposed she had, yet if she thought about the old days at all it was with fondness. She smiled to herself. You only remembered the good bits. Not that there had been many good bits in those days. But she had been determined to lift herself out of her environment and get on in life. She had always known that the back streets of south London were not for her. Hadn't she wanted to be an actress? Whatever happened to that dream?

There were few old residents left by the time the war ended and the square looked a sorry mess. But the years went by and London began to regain its former glory; each residence was bought by a discerning buyer who spent a small fortune restoring it to its original state and adding a few bathrooms on the way. By the Millennium just one remained that had been taken over in the war; the retired gentlewomen's home and that, by general consent, was left alone.

On the point of getting up, Julie lay now for a few more minutes; she loved her thinking-time these days. Long afternoons, winter or summer. Who would have thought she would reach the Millennium? She closed her eyes as she thought of that terrible dome; what a blot on the landscape of her beloved Greenwich, with its beautiful Naval College and the Royal Observatory, Greenwich Park leading on to Blackheath and its village, Croom's Hill, those lovely Georgian houses, the Ranger's house. How often she had stood as a small girl with one foot either side of the meridian . . .

216

Through the window she could see the plane trees in the square. She never tired of looking at them, and thought back to the streets of south London which, despite the poor locality, were often lined with plane trees. She could see the one outside the bedroom she shared with her sister Eileen right now, the wonderful grey bark which peeled to expose such lovely patterns. In summer they would play cricket from one tree to the next, she and the other girls – the boys would never allow the girls to play with them ...

She had almost forgotten the name of the street – but how could she ever forget it? It was imprinted on her memory. Balmoral Street, a royal name ... She must get up or she would drop off and that wouldn't do. She opened her eyes wide and saw the lovely painted French bed, the bed they had managed to keep during that awful time, the dressing table bought by Maurice in Paris after the war, the elegant Lalique lamps, the impressive chandelier – what a difference from that bedroom so long ago. After Maurice died she had gone back once to that street in south London and that had been a mistake she would never repeat.

There had been a name painted on the glass transom of the front door in the long row of new houses that was Balmoral Street, almost obscured by time and weather, what was it ...? Fairview! What sense of the macabre had inspired someone to call it that? The one next door was Sunnyside ...

She got up, slowly taking her time ... How lovely it would be to see them all today ...

Down in the drawing room, that elegant room which had so impressed her all those years ago, she stood looking out again through the long windows, their white shutters pulled back now, through to the square with its

217

newly renovated lawn and plane trees, the little gazebo for use in wet weather generously donated by the residents, the white flowering shrubs which lent such an elegant air to this small oasis, this little piece of London which was so dear to her . . .

She settled herself in her favourite comfortable chair to await the arrival of the family, and as always her eyes moved over to the marble mantelpiece and above it to where hung a small painting of a boy's head – the Rembrandt. The beauty of the quite wonderful drawing moved her every time.

Oh, Maurice, she prayed, wherever you are, I hope you know where it is now . . .